THE NORA NOTEBOOKS

THE TROUBLE WITH FRIENDS

Also by Claudia Mills

The Nora Notebooks #1: The Trouble with Ants
The Nora Notebooks #2: The Trouble with Babies

THE NORA NOTEBOOKS

THE TROUBLE WITH FRIENDS

Book 3

CLAUDIA MILLS

Illustrated by Katie Kath

Alfred A. Knopf   New York

THIS IS A BORZOI BOOK PUBLISHED BY ALFRED A. KNOPF

Knopf, Borzoi Books, and the colophon are registered trademarks of Penguin Random House LLC.

Visit us on the Web! randomhousekids.com

Educators and librarians, for a variety of teaching tools, visit us at RHTeachersLibrarians.com

Library of Congress Cataloging-in-Publication Data
Names: Mills, Claudia, author. | Kath, Katie, illustrator.
Title: The trouble with friends / Claudia Mills ; illustrated by Katie Kath.
Description: First edition. | New York : Alfred A. Knopf, [2017] | Series: The Nora notebooks ; book #3 | Summary: "Nora Alpers, 4th grade scientist, tackles her most difficult subject yet, making friends with someone you have nothing in common with." —Provided by publisher
Identifiers: LCCN 2015034846 | ISBN 978-0-385-39169-6 (trade) | ISBN 978-0-385-39171-9 (pbk.) | ISBN 978-0-385-39170-2 (lib. bdg.) | ISBN 978-0-385-39172-6 (ebook)
Subjects: | CYAC: Friendship—Fiction. | Science—Fiction. | Schools—Fiction.
Classification: LCC PZ7.M63963 Tt 2017 | DDC [Fic]—dc23

The text of this book is set in 12.5-point New Aster.

Printed in the United States of America
March 2017
10 9 8 7 6 5 4 3 2 1

First Edition

For Clara Everett,
with love

THE NORA NOTEBOOKS

THE TROUBLE WITH FRIENDS

"Signs of Spring," Nora Alpers wrote at the top of a blank page in her favorite notebook, where she recorded interesting facts.

Beneath it, she wrote the best sign of spring: "1. ANTS!"

Her fourth-grade teacher, who called himself Coach Joe, had told their class to make lists of the signs of spring they were noticing now that last month's record snowfall was finally melting. Nora knew the other kids in her class would be listing daffodils poking up, warmer weather, softball season beginning. Emma Averill would probably start with the Easter bonnet she had gotten for her cat, Precious Cupcake. Nora had already seen videos of Emma's cat wearing her flower-trimmed straw hat.

Nora's classmates probably hadn't even seen the pavement ants beginning to march across the sidewalk in front of Plainfield Elementary School, foraging for new territory. They didn't notice things like that.

Nora did.

Maybe this spring, she'd follow the ants to their nest. Maybe she'd even catch a glimpse of their queen. Nora had an ant farm at home, filled with ants busy doing fascinating things. But without a queen, her ants died off in months. With a queen, a colony of ants could live forever.

"All right, team!" Coach Joe called to the class. Coach Joe loved sports as much as Nora loved ants. If she was ever a teacher—a professor of myrmecology, the scientific study of ants—she'd start class by saying to her students, "All right, colony!"

She liked the sound of that.

"You can finish your lists later," Coach Joe said. "Huddle time!"

Nora closed her notebook and joined the others for the class meeting on the football-shaped rug in one corner of the classroom. Emma had plopped herself down next to Dunk Edwards, ready to giggle at everything he said or did. Nora could already hear a loud belch from Dunk followed by an appreciative giggle from Emma. Ever since Emma's best friend, Bethy Brink, had moved away last month, Emma's flirting with Dunk had gotten even worse.

"Do you know what day it is?" Coach Joe asked, once everyone was seated.

Nora couldn't figure out what he wanted them to say. Monday? April 11?

"It's opening day," Coach Joe said, "of a brand-new season. Our standardized testing is done for the year"—cheers from the class—"and we're ready to leap into spring. In social studies, we'll be starting our unit on the Civil War, a war that began in April of 1861 and ended in April of 1865."

Dunk switched from burps to the rat-a-tat-tat of imaginary gunfire.

Emma giggled.

Nora perked up as Coach Joe turned to the next subject.

"In science, we're going to be studying botany,

the science of plants, and we'll be making a class garden."

"Can we grow whatever we want?" Brody Baxter asked. Always enthusiastic, Brody sounded ready to grow every kind of plant he could find.

"Each one of you will have part of a row of your own," Coach Joe replied. "You'll need to think of plants that can survive freezing nights and grow fairly quickly. Radishes or lettuce would be good."

Brody's best friend, Mason Dixon, scowled. Mason didn't like any vegetables, or anything to eat other than macaroni and cheese, Cheerios, and Fig Newtons.

"Or peas," Coach Joe added.

Peas! Nora had been reading a wonderful library book about peas. A nineteenth-century Austrian monk named Gregor Mendel had spent his life growing peas in his monastery garden and learning about genes, the biological markers that make all living things what they are. He had discovered the entire science of genetics, all by growing peas.

Nora's parents were both scientists at the university. They had told Nora that, in science, it was important to do experiments over and over again to make sure the same results happened every time. A fact wasn't proven because of how an experiment turned out *once*. Results needed to be *replicated* by scientists all over the world.

Nora could replicate Mendel's experiments with peas she grew herself in the class garden!

She turned back to the huddle.

"In language arts," Coach Joe went on, "we'll be writing poetry."

Elise Fairfield, who loved to write, glowed, and Emma's face wore a dreamy expression. Maybe Emma was envisioning writing a poem about Dunk with rhymes for *belch* and *burp*. What rhymed with *burp*? *Slurp*, maybe. *Dunk slurps. Dunk burps. I'd rather have a bird that chirps.*

Nora's giggle was drowned out by the groans of most of the boys (except for Brody, who never groaned about anything) and some of the girls, too. Nora wasn't looking forward to the poetry unit, either. She liked the way poetry sounded, but she didn't think she'd be good at writing poems herself. Poetry didn't have a clear answer the way science did. How would she know whether she had gotten her poem right?

"Now, team," Coach Joe said, "my challenge is to make poetry fans out of all of you."

Brody beamed. Mason sighed. Dunk grunted. Emma giggled.

Sometimes Nora couldn't help but feel that people were so . . . predictable. Maybe that was what Mendel had proved with his experiments: peas and people had to be whatever they were going to be.

"I'm going to make poetry fans out of *all* of you," Coach Joe repeated. "Poetry is a way of getting you to look at the world with new eyes, and I'm going to see if I can get you to look at poetry with new eyes. Finally, speaking of a new season, new subjects, new plants growing in our new garden, and seeing the world with new eyes, I'm going to give you one more challenge."

Nora waited as Coach Joe took a long, dramatic pause.

"We're at the time of the school year when it's easy to fall into ruts, to do things the way we've always done them—same old, same old, all day long."

Exactly what Nora herself had been thinking!

Dunk was always being so Dunk-ish, Emma so Emma-ish, Mason so Mason-ish, Brody so Brody-ish. Was she always being . . . Nora-ish? Well, she was always thinking about ants. But ants were such a wonderful thing to think about!

Coach Joe continued. "So I want each of you to make a pledge to do something completely new over the course of the next six weeks, something you've never done before."

"Like what?" Nora's closest friend, Amy Talia, asked. Nora guessed that Amy, who loved all kinds of animals (except for ants), would want to get a new pet, which meant a pet in addition to her two dogs, two cats, two rabbits, and two parakeets.

"Anything!" Coach Joe said. "Try a new sport." Nora should have known he'd start off with that one. "See if your parents would let you have some lessons on a new musical instrument. Start learning a foreign language. Spend time with a new friend, preferably someone as different from you as possible. Something big, something small, do anything different at all! See, I made a poem right there." He grinned at his class.

"How long are we supposed to do it?" Tamara

Johnson asked. Tamara, who did jazz dance and hip-hop, would probably want to learn a new form of dance. Maybe ballet?

"Ideally, for a whole month. If it's less, well, that's something, too."

"And then what?" Emma asked.

"Then share your new thing with us in some creative way. Write a poem—yes, by then, you're going to love writing poetry. Make a poster, or a collage, or a video."

"Do we get a prize?" Emma persisted. "If we do the *newest* new thing?"

Coach Joe didn't answer right away. Nora could tell he hadn't thought about prizes. "Well, sure," he finally said. "We can crown a King and Queen of the New. All right, team. Huddle dismissed."

"I hate new things!" Mason muttered as the class filed back to their four-desk pods. Mason was now in Nora's pod; Coach Joe switched the "lineup" of the pods every few weeks. Emma was in Nora's pod, too, even though Emma had already been in Nora's pod earlier this year. Nora liked Emma, but the two of them were definitely as different as different could be.

"Coach Joe said it could be something little," Nora suggested to Mason. "Eat something new."

"I don't like eating new things!"

"Or wear something new. Wear different-colored socks." Mason always wore brown socks.

"I don't like different-colored socks!"

Nora grinned. She was glad she had her new thing picked out: her study of the genetics of peas would be new. Not new to the history of science, of course, because Mendel had already done it, but new to her.

Back at their pod, Emma had taken her seat. "Bethy's moving away to California was a mega-new thing," she said to Nora. "So Bethy did the newest new thing of all. But moving away from your best friend is *too* new, in my opinion."

Nora nodded her head in sympathy.

"What's your new thing going to be?" Emma asked Nora. She had a look in her eyes Nora had never seen before. "Some new project with your nice ants?"

Nora knew Emma hated ants.

"No, I'm going to study a new thing in science," Nora said.

"That sounds like fun!" Emma said. "You're so good at science, Nora."

"What new thing are you going to do?" Nora asked.

Emma might try a new hairstyle. Unlike Nora, Emma adored fixing her blond curly hair.

"I haven't decided yet," Emma said, with an extra-friendly smile.

For some reason, Nora felt uneasy.

"You know what, Nora?" Emma said. "You came over to my house the time I had the fancy tea party for Precious Cupcake."

That was the time Emma's cat had swallowed the ribbon on her fancy kitty dress and had to be rushed to the vet.

"And I've come to your house for the Nellie party."

That was the time Emma had made Nora host a party so the girls could admire her brand-new niece, who was now five weeks old.

"But we've never had any one-on-one time."

This was true. They liked such different things. Nora loved doing experiments on her ants. Emma loved taking videos of her cat. Emma loved stylish clothes. Nora loved nonfiction books. They sat at the same lunch table and hung out with the same group of girls. But they had never really done anything for fun, just the two of them.

"Would you like to come over one day after school this week?" Emma asked. "Or, wait, I have a better idea. Come for a sleepover! Not this weekend, because my grandma is coming to visit. But next weekend. Definitely, next weekend!"

Nora didn't know why she felt strange about

Emma's invitation. It seemed so odd that Emma would ask her today, right this minute, when she had never invited her for a sleepover before.

She smiled weakly and heard herself answer, "Sure."

A terrible suspicion began to form in Nora's brain: Emma's new project was *her*.

The first day of spring is called the vernal equinox. In the Northern Hemisphere it comes around March 20 or 21. But in the Southern Hemisphere everything is backward and it comes around September 22 or 23 because of how Earth tilts on its axis as it orbits the sun. I wonder what an ant's favorite signs of spring would be.

"I'm thinking about a snake," Amy said as the two girls walked home together after school.

"For your new thing?" Nora asked.

Amy nodded, braids bobbing. "But my mom might think a snake is *too* new. For some reason, she hates snakes."

Nora knew how Amy felt. "For some reason, my mom hates *ants*!"

Amy laughed. "What's your new thing?" she asked Nora.

"I've decided to do a new kind of science

experiment. I'm going to experiment on plant genetics in my part of the class garden."

Amy's eyes widened. *Plant genetics* did sound impressive. Then Amy cocked her head to one side.

"Is that new enough?" she asked. "You're already doing science experiments all the time."

"These are different; they're experiments on *plants*," Nora explained. "*Plants* are completely different from *ants*. You're always getting new pets, but a snake will be your first non-mammal or non-bird pet. Reptiles are new for you, and plants are new for me. Plants are even more new compared to ants than snakes are new compared to dogs, cats, rabbits, and parakeets. They're a whole different *kingdom*. I'm going from the animal kingdom to the plant kingdom, and you're still in animal. So mine is extremely new."

Amy's brow wrinkled.

"Everyone is doing the class garden," Amy pointed out. "It's a school thing. Like, we're all going to be writing poetry, but we can't make that be our new thing because it's something we have to do for school."

Nora didn't feel like trying to explain to Amy that

replicating Mendel's experiments on plant genetics was completely different from growing radishes to eat in a salad or pansies to stick in a vase. It was time to change the subject.

"Emma asked if I want to come for a sleepover sometime," she said.

"Like a sleepover party?" Amy asked.

"No," Nora said. "Just her and me."

Amy was so surprised she stopped walking, so Nora had to stop, too.

"*Emma?* Asked *you?* For a *sleepover?* Having a sleepover with Emma is a lot newer than studying plants," Amy said.

"Well," Nora said uncomfortably. "I think . . . You know how Coach Joe said a newness project could be spending time with someone as different from you as possible? And Emma sounded all excited about having the newest project of all? Emma and I are opposites in everything. You know we are. So I think maybe . . ."

Amy waited before replying, as if trying on the idea for size. Then she shrugged. "A sleepover at Emma's would be fun, anyway. Precious Cupcake is soooo adorable. And Emma's snacks are the *best.*"

Would it be fun?

Nora loved *doing* projects. She was always experimenting on her ants, or making a chart of the night sky, or trying to figure out why the Alpers family vacuum cleaner didn't work.

But *being* someone's project? That was a different thing altogether.

Every day when Nora got home from school, her routine was the same:

1. Hang up her coat, if she was wearing a coat.
2. Carry her backpack upstairs to her room and take out her homework, if she had any homework.
3. Check on her ants.

Nora always did the same things in the same order, but her ants always had something new and different to show her. She had never once come home after a whole day away at school and found her ant farm exactly as she had left it. Her ants had dug a new tunnel or hollowed out a new chamber. They had eaten food, transported food, stored food, cleaned up food debris. The world of ants was constantly changing.

Well, unless her ants were dead. Which happened sometimes, in a colony without a queen.

In fact, her colony was drawing closer to the end of its life span right now. There were more dead ants carted off to the ant burial chamber than there were live ants doing the carting.

Nora gazed down at her ants. Even though she knew that dying, like digging, was something ants *did*, she had a pang in her heart each time an entire colony of these busy, bustling, brave, tiny creatures died off.

What if she could find a queen this spring? *That* would be the newest new thing of all.

Dinner at Nora's house was quiet that evening. Nora's older brother, Mark, was off at college, studying electrical engineering. Her older sister, Sarah, lived about an hour away, in Colorado Springs, with her baby, Nellie. Nora's mother was in Budapest, presenting her research on the rings of Saturn at an astronomy conference. So tonight it was just Nora and her biochemist father, eating Indian takeout for the second day in a row at the kitchen table.

"What's new with you?" her father asked as he loaded saag paneer and tandoori chicken onto his plate.

That word again! Nora had never before reflected on how much people cared about new things, greeting each other every single day by asking, "What's *new*?"

"We're going to be planting a class garden," Nora told him.

"Excellent! Is everybody planting the same thing?"

"No, we can plant whatever we want, so long as we pick something that can survive frost and grows pretty fast. I'm going to plant peas."

"Peas?"

"Because of Mendel," Nora explained. "I'm going to try to do the same experiments he did. I'll plant purple-flowered peas and white-flowered peas, and I'll cross-pollinate them—you know, get pollen from one kind of plant and put it on the other kind—and then when they make their seeds, I'll plant *those* seeds, and see if *they* grow up to have purple flowers or white flowers. And I'll either show that Mendel was right about genetics or that he was wrong."

She paused.

"Well, probably I'll show that he was right. Because he did these things in the eighteen hundreds, and if he had been wrong, someone would have probably found it out by now. But it will be interesting to see, won't it?"

"Definitely!" her father said. "I'm not sure, though. . . ." He trailed off.

"Not sure what?" He'd better not be going to say that Mendel's experiments were too hard for a fourth grader.

"You might not have enough time between now and the end of the school year to plant your peas, germinate them, grow them to maturity, cross-pollinate them, harvest the seeds, plant the second generation of seeds, and grow *them* to maturity. It might take too long."

"Dad, that's why Mendel picked peas! Because they grow so fast!"

"Okay," her father agreed. "But *fast* can mean different things to different people. That's all I'm saying."

Mildly annoyed, Nora switched topics. "We're going to be writing poetry, too."

"I know a poem about peas," her father said. "It goes like this: 'I eat my peas with honey; I've done it all my life. It makes the peas taste funny, but it keeps them on the knife.'"

"Dad!" Nora said again.

She knew her parents respected her as a scientist. They told everyone how proud they were of her for being a ten-year-old myrmecologist. But sometimes she had the feeling they didn't take her seriously.

Emma was waiting for Nora on the Plainfield Elementary School playground the next morning before the first bell.

"I brought you a present," she announced.

"Oh," Nora said. "It's not my birthday."

"I know. We talked about that once, remember? You're a Scorpio, and I'm an Aries."

Nora remembered that Emma was interested

in astrology, that fake "science" based on the belief that the personality you had depended on the month you were born in. Nora's mother got irritated when people who didn't know better thought she was an *astrologer* instead of an *astronomer*. As if everyone born between October 23 and November 22 would have the same personality! As if the same predictions could be made about what would happen to millions and millions of people on any given day!

"Why do you have a present for me?" Nora asked. But she had a feeling she already knew the answer.

"It's a 'just because' present," Emma told Nora. She set her backpack on the ground and unzipped the outer compartment.

"Does it have something to do with ants?" Nora asked.

Nora's sister used to like turtles, so everyone kept giving Sarah turtle-shaped earrings, turtle-topped pencils, T-shirts from the Galápagos Islands with pictures of those huge famous tortoises on them (apparently thinking tortoises were the same thing as turtles, or close enough). So far, no one had ever given Nora any ant-themed presents.

"No!" Emma said. "It's something I made. Close your eyes and stick out your hand."

Nora obeyed. She felt Emma's deft fingers tying something around her wrist.

"All right," Emma pronounced. "You can open your eyes now. Ta-da!"

On Nora's left wrist was a thin bracelet made of bright blue and yellow threads knotted together.

"It's a friendship bracelet," Emma said. "And it's the best kind of friendship bracelet because it's the wishing kind. So think of what you're wishing for most in your life right now, and wear this twenty-four/seven until it's totally worn out and falls off *by itself*. You can't *make* it fall off because that would be cheating. And then when it does fall off, your wish will come true. See, I made one for me, too."

Emma held out her own wrist, where a similar pink-and-purple bracelet was fastened.

"Do you like it?" Emma asked.

What could Nora say?

"Sure. Thanks, Emma. That was a nice thing to do for me."

But it would have been nicer if it hadn't been so

painfully obvious that Emma was trying to turn Nora into the best new thing in the class.

"My pleasure!" Emma replied. "So think hard about what you want to wish for!"

If there was anything Nora didn't believe in, it was a wishing bracelet. How could a bunch of knotted threads have the power to alter the course of reality? But suppose it did. What *did* Nora wish for most?

It would be too mean for Nora to use Emma's friendship bracelet to wish that she wasn't so unmistakably Emma's project for Coach Joe's newness challenge.

But if she was honest, that was the first thing that popped into her head on this April morning with a bunch of blue and yellow threads tied to her wrist.

There are many kinds of living things in the world. Scientists put them into different categories, starting with kingdoms, and then going down to things like class, genus, and species. Animals and plants are different kingdoms of living things. Reptiles and mammals are different classes of animals. Dogs and cats are different species of mammals.

The garden, Coach Joe told the class during the morning's huddle, was behind Plainfield Elementary School in a plot of land big enough for each student to get three feet of soil to plant a crop.

"That's not much," Coach Joe said. "So we're going to have to plan carefully. Some of the factors to consider are the time it will take for your crop to grow to maturity, how far apart the plants need to be spaced, how much sun they require, and how tall they are expected to grow. You can find that information here."

He held up a seed catalog with a picture of big, red, ripe tomatoes on the front cover.

"All right, team, back to the dugout." That's what Coach Joe called their pods, when he was in an extra-sporty mood. "I have a catalog for each pod, so take one with you."

Nora let her pod mates look first. She already knew she was planting peas.

Thomas W., the quietest kid in the whole class, picked radishes. Nora watched as he marked a green circle around one of the half dozen varieties on the radish page. He didn't actually speak aloud the word *radish*.

"Why did you pick radishes?" Nora wanted to know.

He shrugged without speaking.

Mason picked radishes, too. "Since I hate all vegetables equally," he said, "I might as well plant radishes. They're small, at least. So there'll be less to go to waste when I don't eat them."

"I'm going to grow flowers," Emma said. "And I'm going to talk to them to make them grow better. Did you know plants grow better if you talk to them?"

"No," Nora said. "Flowers don't have ears. Flowers don't have brains. So flowers can't hear human speech."

She didn't want to be rude, but she had already stopped herself from commenting on zodiac signs and wishing bracelets.

"I heard it on a television program," Emma said, as if that made it true. "I did!" She turned back to the catalog, sighing over the page of pansies. "Pansies have the sweetest faces!"

She held the catalog open so Nora could see. The markings on the flowers did sort of look like two dark eyes, a yellow nose, and an open mouth. But it was a stretch, at best, to call that a face.

The pictures showed pansies in different colors: purples, pinks, blues, yellows.

"Which one are you going to get?" Nora asked.

"I don't know. Maybe Sunrise." Emma read aloud the catalog description: "'All the hues of early dawn.' Or 'Ocean Breeze. Shifting shades of sea and sky.'"

"You're picking them based on their names?" Nora asked.

Emma nodded. "Shifting shades of sea and sky.

All the hues of early dawn. Early dawn. Sea and sky. Okay, shifting shades of sea and sky."

Across the room, Nora could hear Brody saying, "I want to grow radishes *and* spring greens *and* Asian greens *and* baby carrots. If the carrots take all summer to grow, I can come back and water them, right? And wait to pick them until they're completely ready."

Amy wandered over to check on Nora. Coach Joe didn't mind quiet visits from one pod to another.

"I'm doing radishes," Amy reported. "My whole pod is doing radishes. They're fast, they're easy, and my rabbits adore them. Did you pick out your peas?"

"No." Nora hadn't had a chance yet because Emma was too busy exclaiming over the names and faces of pansies.

"Here, Nora." Emma offered her the catalog. "You can pick now. Are there any plants you could grow that your ants would adore?"

There were things Nora could grow that her ants would *eat*. For a moment, she felt guilty she hadn't even thought about ant preferences in choosing her crop. She wasn't being as considerate of her ants as Amy was of her rabbits. But she couldn't say there was anything she could grow that her ants would *adore.*

"I think they'd like peas," Nora said. She couldn't imagine they wouldn't.

She turned to the pea page of the catalog.

There were so many kinds! If only she knew exactly what Gregor Mendel had grown. Sugar Daddy peas? Goliath peas? Super Sugar Snap peas? She wished the catalog had pictures of the pea flowers as well as of the final pods plump with the peas themselves. Were the flowers on Sugar Daddy peas purple or white? How could she breed for flower color if she didn't even know what color flowers she was buying?

Then her eyes fell on the Maestro pea facts.

Sun: Full sun.

Height: 26 inches.

Time to maturity: 61 days.

Sixty-one days? Two *months*?

Quickly she scanned the peas on the page. The shortest time given was fifty-five days. Or in other words, forever.

Either Gregor Mendel had grown some special,

super-speedy peas or *fast* did mean different things to different people.

She hated when she was wrong and her parents were right.

If Nora planted peas, she'd be eleven or twelve before she had planted and harvested enough generations of peas to find out if Mendel had been correct about plant genetics. She'd be all the way to middle school!

So much for plants as her new thing. Amy had been right about that, too. Well, if the peas had worked out, they would have been new enough. Or maybe not. Nora would have been one of thousands of scientists who had copied Gregor Mendel, and nothing special at all.

She might as well grow radishes like Thomas, Mason, Brody, Amy, and, apparently, half of Coach Joe's class.

But she would not grow pansies picked on the basis of a poetic name. And she would not talk to her plants as they grew.

That much she knew for sure.

Nora was hardly in the mood for poetry during language arts time.

Coach Joe had a poem up on the board for the class to read. It was a poem about spring by someone named e. e. cummings.

"Why is his name spelled like that?" Brody wanted to know.

"He was born Edward Estlin Cummings," Coach Joe said. "So that's what *e. e.* stands for. You'll notice that the poem itself has hardly any capital letters in it. None of the lines begin with a capital, do they?"

Nora studied the poem. What Coach Joe had said was true.

"What did he have against capital letters?" Mason asked, as if relieved that someone else had a negative attitude against something most people liked.

"Maybe it wasn't that he had a grudge against capitals, but that lowercase letters had some special appeal for him," Coach Joe answered. "Why do you think that might be?"

"He wanted to be different," one kid said.

"He didn't want to have to remember where to

put the capitals," Dunk suggested. Dunk was notoriously lazy.

Elise was the best writer in the class, so when she raised her hand to offer an idea, Nora was interested to hear it.

"It sort of looks kidlike," Elise said. "Little kids might not know how to write with capitals. Capitals look big and official. Without capitals, the poem looks more little and friendly."

"Good, good," Coach Joe said.

He read the poem aloud. Nora didn't understand the point of it. There was a lot about a balloon man whistling "far and wee." Why would someone want to write a poem about that? And he used strange phrases like "mud-luscious" and "puddle-wonderful."

"The poem has a lot of signs of spring in it," Coach Joe said. "What are some of them?"

People raised their hands to point out mud and puddles, kids playing hopscotch and jump rope, the balloon man whistling.

"The balloon man isn't a *spring* thing," Nora said. "You can have balloons any time of year. So that's not really a sign of spring."

"I think it is," Elise said. "I don't think the balloon man would be out selling balloons in the middle of winter. And the way he keeps whistling far and wee—it's as if he's happy it's spring and he can be outside with his big bunch of balloons."

Well, Elise knew more about poetry than Nora did, that was for sure.

Coach Joe pointed out that e. e. cummings used several of the five senses in the poem. You could *see* the balloon man and *hear* his far-and-wee whistle and *feel* the squelch of the mud and the splash of the puddle.

"All right, team," Coach Joe said. "Take your list of signs of spring and work on putting them into a springtime poem the way e. e. cummings did. Use as many senses as possible. And see if you can make up any phrases of your own like 'mud-luscious' and 'puddle-wonderful.' Okay, play ball!"

Nora hadn't added anything else to her Signs of Spring list. Ants were enough. She had already filled one of her many notebooks with fascinating facts about ants. Surely she could write a poem about them.

But writing a poem turned out to be harder

than writing a list of facts, Nora found out as she sat chewing on her pencil and wondering how to begin. Much harder. How could you take facts and make them sound poetic instead of just factual? She could think of words that rhymed with *ants: dance, pants, plants.* But e. e. cummings had written his poem without using rhyme. Maybe she could sort of copy his, but stick in ants instead of a balloon man. She could write without capitals and use the word *wee* to mean *little.*

After a few minutes, she read over what she had written.

> in just April
> when the snow is wet-melting
> and the pavement is sun-steamy,
> ~~the ants come marching~~

Nora crossed out that last line. She was already copying e. e. cummings. She wasn't going to copy "The Ants Go Marching" as well.

> the ants come out
> wee but many
> wee but mighty
> wee and hungry
> ready for spring

Seeds come in different sizes, shapes, and colors. Inside every seed lives a tiny plant, or embryo. So if you put a bunch of radish seeds in your hand, you are really holding hundreds of radishes. All seeds need water, oxygen, and the right temperature in order to germinate, or begin to grow. Some seeds germinate better in light. Some germinate better in darkness.

Nora's mother returned from Budapest on Friday, and Nora's sister, Sarah, and Nora's niece, Nellie, came over on Saturday morning to spend the weekend. Sarah's husband, Jeff, wouldn't be home from his tour of duty as an air force pilot until June.

As soon as Nora collected Nellie from Sarah's arms, she noticed something amazing.

Nora smiled at Nellie.

And Nellie smiled back!

"She smiled at me," Nora crowed. But maybe

it wasn't a real smile. She had learned that some-times when babies look as if they're smiling, it might be a reflex reaction to rumbles in their digestive systems. But at six weeks old, Nellie wasn't a newborn anymore.

"Was that a real smile or a gas smile?" Nora asked, worried she had crowed too soon.

"A real smile," Sarah replied, with an equally big smile of her own.

Nora's father and mother each took turns holding Nellie, smiling huge smiles at her, and getting toothless grins in return.

It was odd to think of smiling—just smiling—as a new thing for Nellie: a thing she once hadn't been able to do but could do now.

"Nellie's doing something new every day," Sarah said, as if reading Nora's thoughts.

"Like what?" Nora wanted to know.

"Like, she can hold her head up so well by herself these days. She slept six hours straight last night. And when I read to her, she listens."

"How do you know she's listening?" Nora had to ask.

"A mother just knows," Sarah said serenely. "I

brought some of her books. I'll read one to her and you'll see."

Nora's mother handed Nellie back to Sarah, and Sarah tucked her into the crook of her arm. With her free hand, she fumbled in her overstuffed diaper bag and produced a sturdy board book.

"'Hey diddle diddle, the cat and the fiddle, the cow jumped over the moon. The little dog laughed to see such a sight, and the dish ran away with the spoon,'" Sarah read.

Was Nellie listening or not? Not, Nora decided. The baby screwed up her face and began to cry. Or maybe she *had* been listening, and didn't like poetry. Or didn't like this particular poem. The poem was misleading, in Nora's opinion. It would give Nellie wrong ideas about cats, cows, the moon, dogs, dishes, and silverware, all in six lines.

"Maybe she doesn't like poetry," Nora suggested.

"All babies like poetry," Sarah said. "They like the sound of it, the music of the lines, the rhythms and the rhymes."

Nora remembered something Coach Joe had said to the class on Friday. They were supposed to ask their family members what their favorite poems were. Nora wondered if her parents had favorite poems. They were scientists. Her father might have a favorite molecule. Her mother had a favorite planet (Saturn), and she might even have a special fondness for one of its rings. Sarah, who was a geologist when she wasn't home on maternity leave, might have a favorite rock. Of course, Nora had a favorite insect: ants.

But a favorite poem?

"Coach Joe said I'm supposed to ask you what your favorite poem is," she said.

A dreamy look came over her parents' faces.

"'How do I love thee?'" her mother said, obviously quoting from a poem, as people today—except for Elise—didn't say *thee*.

"'Let me count the ways,'" her father replied.

"'I love thee to the depth and breadth and height,'" her mother continued.

"'My soul can reach, when feeling out of sight . . .'"

"'For the ends of being and ideal grace. . . .'"

At least Sarah looked bewildered, too.

"Elizabeth Barrett Browning," their mother explained. "One of the *Sonnets from the Portuguese* she wrote for her husband, Robert Browning. Your father and I would send lines of it back and forth to each other on postcards when we were first falling in love."

Well, being in love might lead two scientists to quote poetry to each other day and night.

But then her mother said, "Edna St. Vincent Millay. Emily Dickinson. Denise Levertov. I loved them all. I still love them. I wanted to be a poet just like them when I grew up."

"But you became a scientist instead," Nora reminded her.

"There's poetry in the skies, too," her mother said. "And I turned out to be better at appreciating other people's poetry than I am at writing it myself."

"Do *you* have a favorite poem?" Nora asked her father. Maybe it was that poem about the peas he had quoted the other night at dinner?

"Robert Frost," he said without a moment's hesitation. "'Two roads diverged in a yellow wood. . . .'"

"Sarah?" Nora asked.

"Dr. Seuss! *Oh, the Places You'll Go!* That's poetry, too. I've already read it to Nellie a hundred times."

Nora had definitely learned something new about her family, this Saturday morning.

Nora walked over to Mason's house Sunday afternoon, when Nellie and Sarah were taking a nap together. She found Mason and Brody in the backyard, throwing a ball for their three-legged dog, Dog. Mason and Brody were not only best friends, they were also next-door neighbors and co-owners of Dog. They loved him equally, but he lived at Mason's house because of Brody's father's allergies.

"I've done seven new things already!" Brody greeted Nora.

Brody often said things that would have been braggy if someone else had said them, but Brody couldn't help being excited about everything. That was just the way he was.

"On Monday, I ate an artichoke. On Tuesday, I took a cold shower, because my sisters had used up the hot water. On Wednesday, Cammie taught me how to do a cartwheel."

He paused to demonstrate. It was more accurate

to say Cammie had taught him how to *try* to do a cartwheel. His legs weren't upright enough. They flipped over in more of a flop-wheel.

"On Thursday—I don't remember what new thing I did on Thursday, but I know I did one. On Friday, I learned to count to ten in Spanish. *Uno, dos, tres, cuatro, cinco, seis, siete, ocho, nueve, diez.* On Saturday, I learned to count to ten in German. *Eins, zwei, drei, vier, fünf, sechs, sieben, acht, neun, zehn.*"

Nora was impressed that Brody had already filled almost an entire week with nonstop newness.

"And *today*," Brody said. "Are you ready to hear what new thing I did *today*?"

"Sure," Nora said.

"*Today*," Brody said, "I watched a sad movie, and I was sad for a whole hour. I've never been sad for a whole entire hour before."

Nora laughed.

"Did you pick your new thing?" she asked Mason. He shook his head.

"I guess I could learn to count to ten in French," he said. "My mother took French in high school, and she could teach me. But I don't think that would be a big enough new thing if it was the only

44

new thing I did. I'd probably have to learn how to count to ten *and* learn how to say, 'What's your name? My name is Mason' and 'How are you?' and 'please' and 'thank you' and a bunch of other things. And if any real French person heard me, he'd be mad I butchered his beautiful language. What about you?"

Nora had known the question was coming.

"I had a new thing picked out, a new experiment I was going to do in the class garden, but it didn't work out. It had to do with peas, and they take too long to grow, so now it's radishes for me, like everyone else."

Maybe Nora could find a new radish-growing experiment in Coach Joe's big book of science fair experiments. But her heart wasn't in it.

"Nellie smiled at me. That was new. But it's more of a new thing for Nellie than it is for me."

"You and I are more like Dog," Mason said as he tossed the battered tennis ball the hundredth time. "Dog doesn't say, 'I need a new ball to fetch! I want to fetch a squeaky toy! I want to fetch a toy that lights up and plays "Pop Goes the Weasel"!' He *likes* fetching the same ball over and over again. Right, Dog?"

Dog laid the ball at Mason's feet, panting with happiness.

Nora couldn't tell if Mason's comparing her to Dog was comforting or not.

Amy called Nora on Sunday night.

"Bad news," Amy said. "My mother said no to the snake. I knew she would. It's sad when older people are so closed-minded about new ideas. And my mom's only forty."

"I'm sorry," Nora said.

"You don't suppose . . ." Amy's voice trailed off.

Nora already knew what Amy was going to say.

"I'd provide the frozen mice to feed it with. And I'd get a good lid for the terrarium so it can't get out," Amy promised.

"No," Nora said. "My mom is closed-minded, too, when it comes to snakes. She's not going to want a snake in our house."

Nora didn't *know* that. But she suspected it strongly.

And, if truth be told, when it came to feeding frozen mice to a pet snake, Nora was a bit closed-minded herself.

Newborn babies can give smiles when they are asleep. But babies have their first real social smiles at other people when they are 6 or 8 weeks old. A social smile is a smile in response to somebody else's smile. Just like Nellie smiled at me.

5

The pre-dug furrows in Coach Joe's class garden were neatly measured off with strings stretched across them from posts at each end. Name tags clipped to the strings with clothespins marked off each student's section of soil.

Nora had thought the radish people would be together, but on Monday morning, she found herself outside in the garden, positioned between Brody's everything seeds on one side and Emma's pansies on the other.

Even before her seeds were planted, Emma was already talking to them.

"Little seeds, today is a big day for you!" she crooned to the picture of the purple-hued pansies on the front of the Ocean Breeze seed packet. "Today you enter the earth! Today you experience sun and soil and water! Today your journey begins!"

Even more unscientific than talking to *plants*, in Nora's view, was talking to *seeds*.

"You haven't planted them yet!" Nora told Emma.

"Lots of mothers talk to their babies before they're born," Emma replied, clutching the package of seeds to her chest as if it was an infant in need of cuddling. "I bet your sister read to Nellie during her pregnancy. Ask her."

Nora had a feeling Emma was right on this one. If Sarah had read Dr. Seuss to Nellie a hundred times already, some of the reading may have taken place before Nellie's birth.

She heard Brody whispering to his seeds as he put each one into the ground, evidently inspired by Emma.

"Grow, little carrots! Grow, little salad greens!"

One row ahead of Nora, Amy turned around and

flashed Nora a grin of amusement at Emma's and Brody's seed conversations.

Mason sprinkled radish seeds into his furrow, next to Amy's.

"I bet mine don't sprout," Mason predicted. "And what's going to stop rabbits from hopping in to eat them if they do?"

Coach Joe overheard Mason's question. "We'll fence around the garden next week, before the seeds start germinating. The fence will be high enough to keep out rabbits. I don't know about deer."

Mason brightened at the thought that even if his radishes weren't gobbled by rabbits, they had a good chance of being devoured by deer.

Dunk was planting pumpkins. Apparently he had tuned out when Coach Joe had told the class to plant a crop with a short enough life cycle that it could be harvested before school ended. Dunk's pumpkins wouldn't be ripe until close to Halloween. Maybe, like Brody, Dunk planned to water them through the summer. Probably Brody would actually water his carrots. Dunk's pumpkins didn't have a chance.

"They're going to be *this* big!" Dunk shouted, holding up his arms as wide as they could reach. "If I dropped one on your puny, scrawny radishes, it'd be like an atom bomb exploding. Pow! Crash! Kaboom!"

Leave it to Dunk to turn a class garden into nuclear warfare. He was clearly ready to film his own horror movie, *Attack of the Killer Pumpkins.*

Nora looked at the notes she had written in her special notebook in preparation for planting her radishes. She wanted to do something scientific with them, even if it didn't count as her new thing. Why miss out on the chance to contribute something to the world's storehouse of knowledge?

She had sorted the tiny seeds, as best she could, into four piles. One group she had frozen overnight. One she had baked for half an hour in the oven. One she had briefly microwaved. The other was her control group, the normal group to which she had done nothing.

Exactly how would temperature extremes affect germination? Would radiation from the microwave have any effect?

It was on the minimal side as a contribution to science.

But right now it was all Nora had.

"Little seeds, I bless you!" Emma intoned. "Little seeds, go forth and grow!"

"Go forth and die is more like it," Mason muttered to the furrow where he had dumped his radishes.

"Pow! Pow! Pow!" Dunk shouted as he dropped each pumpkin seed.

Nora tuned them out, concentrating on placing her frozen seeds, baked seeds, microwaved seeds, and control-group seeds carefully into the waiting earth.

"So is this weekend still okay?" Emma asked Nora as they headed toward the cafeteria for lunch. The other girls in their lunch-table group—Tamara, Elise, and Amy—were farther back in line.

"For the sleepover," Emma added, as if Nora could possibly have forgotten.

Nora considered making up some excuse. But she wasn't the type of person to tell an outright lie.

"I'm going to be pretty busy this weekend," she said.

She was always busy: looking after her ant

farm, doing homework, reading library books on volcanoes or fossils of the Cretaceous Period. On Wednesday afternoons, she volunteered with Amy at the animal shelter. On Thursday afternoons, when the new season began this week, she'd be at softball practice with Tamara and Elise, with Saturday morning or afternoon games.

Emma pushed out her lower lip in a pout.

"Busy doing what?" she demanded. "Whatever it is, I bet it doesn't take up every minute of every day all weekend. You have to sleep, right? Everyone sleeps. So you might as well sleep at my house. Saturday night? Come at six? For make-your-own pizza? Precious Cupcake *loves* make-your-own pizza."

"Okay," Nora said. "Saturday could work for me."

Maybe if she had the sleepover with Emma, Emma's project would be done, and they could go back to being regular non-project friends again.

"You don't need to bring a sleeping bag," Emma said. "Just bring yourself! Well, and your pj's. And a toothbrush!"

They had reached the cafeteria.

Emma flashed Nora a huge smile as she picked up her tray.

"This is going to be great!"

It had been chilly for the past few days, but it was warm enough that afternoon that Nora took off her sweater and tied it around her waist as she walked home with Amy.

"What do you think would be a good name for a snake, if I get one?" Amy asked. "I'm thinking about *Fred*."

"Do you think your mother's going to change her mind?"

"I'm working on her. I've been putting snake pictures on the refrigerator. I read that if people have a phobia—you know, a weird fear of something—they can get over it if you help them get used to it in itty-bitty ways. So looking at snake pictures can help a person not mind seeing a real-life snake."

"Is it working?"

"Not yet. It would work better if she didn't keep taking the pictures down and throwing them away. What's that on your wrist?"

The question caught Nora by surprise. She looked down at Emma's bracelet on her arm, newly bare on this spring day.

"That's not a friendship bracelet, is it?" Amy asked.

"Well, sort of. Emma gave it to me."

"Emma?" Then Amy nodded with understanding. "Oh, I get it: the newness project."

"She told me I was supposed to make a wish on it," Nora said.

"Did you?"

"Not yet," Nora said.

The wish Nora had almost made—that Emma would stop making Nora her project—didn't really count. So she still had a wish waiting for her.

That is, if she believed in wishes.

Many things can cause seeds to have trouble germinating. Overwatering causes a plant to not have enough oxygen. (Like when people drown.) Planting seeds too deep in the ground makes them have to work too hard before they reach the soil surface. Underwatering causes the plant to not have enough moisture to start the germination process. It's really pretty amazing that any seeds germinate at all.

6

After school on Wednesday, Amy's mother picked up Amy and Nora for their weekly volunteering at the Plainfield animal shelter. Usually they walked dogs on the loop trail behind the shelter, to give the confined animals much-needed exercise. But sometimes they sat inside and cuddled cats.

Today was a cat-cuddling day.

In the cat visitation room off the main lobby, Nora sat with a plump ginger-colored cat on her lap, while Amy amused a scrawnier black kitty with a feather fastened to the end of a long string. Nora's cat purred with contentment, sounding like a boat's motor at full throttle. Amy's cat stalked the feather as intently as if it had been a whole tasty bird. Amy's mother sat nearby, reading a book; kids under fifteen couldn't volunteer without a parent, but the parent didn't have to do anything, just be there to supervise.

"Cassidy is so sweet," Amy said, about the cat purring in Nora's lap.

"He is," Nora agreed, stroking Cassidy's soft orange fur and scratching gently behind his ears.

"You could adopt him," Amy said. "For your new thing. You *could*."

Nora's hand paused mid-stroke as she considered Amy's idea.

Could she adopt a cat? *Should* she?

Her parents had always seemed neutral on pets. They traveled a lot for work, off to conferences here and conferences there, so they never sought out pets themselves. But now that Nora was old enough to take full responsibility for a pet, they'd probably say yes if she asked, especially for a pet as sweet and comforting as Cassidy. And Nora would

never let any cat of hers be dressed in costumes or star in cat videos, as Precious Cupcake did.

Would her ants mind?

She couldn't in all honesty say they would. Ants didn't get jealous. That wasn't what ants did.

Yet Nora felt disloyal at the thought of her ants displaced in her affections by a mammal pet, a pet that could sleep in her bed, come meowing to the door when she returned from school, communicate with her by sound and gesture, and stay alive for more than a few short weeks or months.

They might not be jealous of a cat, but Nora felt jealous on their behalf.

Amy was able to divide her love among dogs, cats, rabbits, parakeets; she even had enough love left over to give to a snake.

Nora was more of a one-species lover.

"No," Nora finally said. "Cassidy's the best cat ever, he truly is. But I'm going to stick with ants."

Yet when the animal shelter man came to collect Cassidy at the end of their volunteer slot, Nora surrendered him with a pang.

Ants weren't soft.

Ants weren't cuddly.

Cassidy was soft *and* cuddly.

Ants didn't purr when you held them.

Cassidy did.

The first softball practice of the season was after school on Thursday. If only Nora hadn't played softball last year, this could have been her new thing.

Tamara and Elise were on the team, too. Tamara, who loved dancing, played second base with agility and grace. Even when she struck out, her swings were elegant, not awkward and flailing. Elise had a great throwing arm, but she had a tendency to daydream out in right field, as likely to be making up a poem in her head as to be catching a fly ball.

Nora considered herself to be a pretty good shortstop. She was quick and strong, but her best trait, in her own opinion, was that she was good at paying attention. Someone who spent as much time as Nora did studying ants scurrying and digging knew how to watch.

The softball coach was a woman named Coach Josie, Jo for short. It was strange that Nora had two Coach Jo(e)s in her life.

The girls partnered for a throwing and catching drill. Nora threw a straight, hard pitch into Tamara's well-positioned glove.

"Nice, Nora, nice," Coach Jo said.

Nora had a sudden idea.

"Coach Jo?" she said as the coach stood behind her. "Do you think you could try me as pitcher this spring?"

That would be a new thing!

Coach Jo pulled off her cap and ruffled her short, spiky hair in an uncomfortable way.

"Well, Nora," she said, "you might have potential on the mound. But I already have Abby and Eleanor in that position, and I need your fast reflexes as shortstop. Maybe later in the season we could shift things up a bit, though."

Later in the season would be too late.

"That's okay," Nora said. "I mean, I understand completely."

She missed the next throw from Tamara and had to dart after the ball as it rolled toward the bleachers.

Maybe she should get a cat after all?

No. Amy and Emma were cat lovers. Mason and Brody were dog lovers. Nora was an ant lover.

All she could do was hope very hard that she would end up proving something new and startling about the effects of microwaving on radish seeds.

Or that having a sleepover with Emma was new enough to make up for being an ant-loving, no-other-pet-owning, plain old shortstop.

"Haiku," Coach Joe said during the poetry huddle on Friday. "Who knows what a haiku is?"

Lots of hands went up. Coach Joe called on Elise, perhaps because she was recognized as the class poetry expert.

"There are three lines," Elise reported. "The first line has five syllables, the next line has seven, and the last line has five. So seventeen syllables total."

"Correct!" Coach Joe said. "Haiku is an ancient form of poetry from Japan. We're going to be writing haiku today."

The groans were muted this time. Seventeen syllables wasn't too terrible an assignment.

Nora had written haiku before, in third grade. It was satisfying to count the syllables in her head,

5-7-5, like solving an equation in math: $5 + 7 + 5 = 17$. Simple, straightforward, mathematical. Add it up, and there was your poem.

"But," Coach Joe went on, "I'm going to say something that may surprise you. It's not the number of syllables that is most important here. It's the idea of taking some experience and condensing it into a tiny package. That means choosing and selecting which details matter most. Often haiku poets wrote about nature or the changing seasons. They looked very hard at something in nature and tried to see it anew, as if for the first time. But you can write about any subject in your haiku, so long as you present it in a few carefully chosen details."

Coach Joe read some examples of haiku by famous Japanese poets and by actual kids. Then he sent the students to their pods to write.

"We'll come back to share in fifteen minutes," he told the class.

How could Coach Joe think it would take fifteen minutes to write seventeen syllables? Practically one minute for each one!

But back at her desk, Nora spent a few of her minutes staring down at a blank page in her notebook.

She knew she'd write about ants, of course.

She liked the idea of a tiny poem about a tiny creature.

But *which* seventeen syllables should she write?

When it was time to share, Nora wasn't sure she liked what she had written. But it was the best she could do to capture the wonderfulness of ants in three short lines.

"All right," Coach Joe said, "who wants to go first?"

To Nora's surprise, the first hand in the air was Mason's.

"Mason, my friend," Coach Joe said. "Do share your haiku with us."

"'How I Feel About Poetry,'" Mason read from his sheet. "That's my title. Syllables in the title don't count, right?"

"Right," Coach Joe agreed.

Mason read his poem.

HOW I FEEL ABOUT POETRY
by Mason

No no no no no
No no no no no no no
No no no no no

Everyone laughed, including Coach Joe.

"Very clever, Mason," Coach Joe said. "But I hope that in a few weeks, you'll want to revise your poem to this."

HOW I FEEL ABOUT POETRY
by Coach Joe

No. No. No. No. No.
Well, maybe. Maybe. Maybe.
Wait. . . . Yes? Yes? Yes. Yes!

Lots of kids wanted to read now. Seventeen-syllable poems kept zinging through the air.

HIP-HOP
by Tamara

When I start to dance
My feet have their own ideas.
My body follows.

PRECIOUS CUPCAKE
by Emma

My cat is the best.
White, soft, fluffy, blue eyes, tail.
She is the cutest.

HAPPINESS
by Brody

It feels like soda
Fizzing up out of the can
All over the floor.

CROCUS
by Elise

Before snow is gone
Green shoots poke through. Yellow blooms,
Then purple. Then pink.

PUMPKINS
by Dunk

Radishes are dumb.
Lettuce is dumb, too. Pumpkins
Rule the world. Kaboom!

WHEN I GROW UP
by Amy

When I'm a mom some-
Day, my kids can have ten snakes
And I'll say, "Hooray!"

ANT

by Nora

The ant is smaller
Than the cracker crumb. But she
Carries it so far.

Even if I'm not getting a cat, I can look up facts about cats. There are about 600 million domestic cats in the world. There are approximately 85.8 million pet cats in the United States compared to 77.8 million dogs. About 35 percent of households in America own a cat. But not mine.

7

"I was thinking," Nora said to her parents that evening at dinner. "I might like to get a musical instrument and start taking some lessons."

Her father choked on his ice water.

Her mother paused her meatball-laden fork halfway to her mouth.

Nora told them about Coach Joe's newness challenge, leaving out her doomed hope for making her new thing be replicating Mendel's results about the genetics of peas.

"I have a clarinet from high school band around

here somewhere," Nora's mother said. "I could try to find it and show you the basics. I'd hate to go to the trouble and expense of getting a whole new instrument, finding a teacher, paying for lessons, if—well, Nora, do you really want to learn a musical instrument, or are you doing this to get the new thing over with? I can't see you playing the clarinet, somehow."

"I *might* want to play it," Nora said.

If her scientist mother had played the clarinet in high school, and had loved poetry, why would she think her scientist daughter might not want to branch out a bit? Maybe Nora's ants would like the sound of clarinet music. They were more likely to enjoy clarinet music, in Nora's opinion, than Emma's pansies were likely to enjoy Emma's singing.

Half an hour later, Nora's mother appeared from the attic, a smudge of dirt on one cheek, a cobweb in her hair, and a clarinet case clutched in her hand.

"I hope it's playable," she said. "I can't think of any reason it wouldn't be. Oh, maybe the reeds."

Nora must have looked bewildered, because her mother explained, "The reed is this little bit of wood you put on the mouthpiece. Maybe reeds go bad after thirty years? There's only one way to find out."

She showed Nora how to suck on the reed to moisten it: mildly gross. Then she inserted the reed onto the clarinet mouthpiece and attached the mouthpiece to the slim, dark body of the clarinet.

"All right," she said. "Now I have to see if I can play this thing. Maybe it's like riding a bike, and however many years go by since you rode one last, you hop back on and go."

It wasn't. Or rather, it was more like riding a wobbly bike and falling off a lot. Nora's mother finally managed to play "Twinkle, Twinkle, Little Star"—an appropriate choice for an astronomer. It was even an appropriate choice for an astronomer who studied planets, given that most people, when they wished upon the first star of the evening, were wishing instead upon the planet Venus.

"Now you try it." Nora's mother held out the clarinet to Nora.

She helped Nora position her fingers over the holes and place her mouth on the reed and blow.

The high-pitched shriek that followed would have sent Nora's ants scurrying to their deepest tunnel. It would have made listening radishes wither and die.

Nora tried again. She couldn't honestly say the second time was any better.

"It sounds terrible for every beginner," Nora's mother reassured her as her father removed his hands from his ears. "Maybe we *should* get you some lessons. I remember how to play it—sort of— but I don't remember how poor Mr. McGinness taught us to do it."

"Actually," Nora said, "I don't think I want to play the clarinet."

Both her parents looked relieved.

Nora's ant colony was dying off. There was no doubt about it.

Upstairs in her room after dinner, she tried not to mind seeing their stiff, small bodies piling up in the ant burial chamber. That was a part of the fascination of having an ant farm, to see the cycle of life unfold before her eyes. When golden leaves fell off the aspen trees in autumn and the branches stood bare, it wasn't a sad thing. That was what aspen trees *did*.

But Nora's ant farm didn't get to experience the full cycle of life, because she didn't have a queen. With no ant queen, she had no ant eggs, no ant babies, no young ants to grow up to replace the other worker ants as they lived, toiled, and died.

If only Nora had a queen!

That's what she should have wished for with Emma's friendship bracelet, still fastened around her wrist, frayed now after almost two weeks of play and much scrubbing.

Did you have to make the wish at the time you got the bracelet? Or could you make the wish later? Or change your first wish into a better wish once you realized your true heart's desire?

Nora couldn't help touching the bracelet lightly with the fingertips of her other hand.

"I wish I could find a queen," she said aloud, into her empty room.

Just in case.

"A sleepover?" Nora's mother asked as she set a bowl of yogurt, blueberries, and granola in front of Nora on Saturday morning. "Yes, of course you can go. That sounds like a lot of fun."

"But . . ." Nora loaded up a first spoonful with the exact right amount of blueberries. "We'll probably stay up late and not get enough sleep."

Would they? What would they stay up late *doing,* given how completely different their interests were?

Nora had a hopeful thought: maybe Precious Cupcake would sit purring on her lap the way Cassidy had. But Emma's cat probably purred only for Emma.

Nora's mother chuckled. "I'm supposed to be the one worrying about how much you'll sleep, not you. You can take a nap Sunday afternoon if you're tired. We don't have any plans as a family for Sunday."

Nora sighed.

"What's going on?" her mother asked then. "Is there some reason you don't want to go?"

"It's just . . . Emma and I . . . I mean, she's nice and everything, but we don't have very much in common."

She thought about telling her mother that Emma was just doing this to win a prize for having the newest new project of all. But it was such a sad thing to have to say.

"That's why I'm so pleased you're doing this," Nora's mother said. "It's good to get out of our comfort zones once in a while. That's how we stretch and grow."

Nora glared at her mother. *Why don't you study a different planet for a change, then?* she wanted to say. *Instead of Saturn, Saturn, Saturn all the time, why don't you study Mercury? Or Mars?*

But there was no point in saying anything.

Emma called Nora mid-afternoon.

"I have good news and bad news," Emma announced. "Which do you want to hear first?"

"Good news," Nora said. She could use some good news right about now.

"I thought up the best game for us to play at the sleepover. I'll give you one clue. To play it, we need ten bottles of nail polish in all different colors. And not ordinary ones like Pretty in Pink or Scarlet Letter or Lavender Bouquet or Purple Passion. Way-out ones, like Green Means Go or Yellow Rose of Texas."

Emma sounded genuinely enthusiastic, as if she wanted to play this game more than anything in the world, and wanted to play it with Nora. But Nora knew Emma really wanted to play this game with Bethy, who was a thousand miles away.

"Plus sparkly ones!" Emma added. "And ones that light up in the dark!"

"What's the bad news?" Nora made herself ask.

"It's bad," Emma said, as if the warning would help Nora brace herself for what she was about to say next.

"What is it?"

It couldn't be too bad if Emma sounded so excited about the nail polish game. It couldn't be anything terrible happening to Precious Cupcake. There would be no news good enough to make up for that.

"My dad didn't know tonight was our sleepover, so he got tickets for my parents and my sister and me to go to a play in Denver. We're going to have to postpone the sleepover for another week. Is that okay? Say it's okay!"

Relief made Nora feel giddy.

"It's definitely okay!" It was better than okay. "In fact—"

"So next Saturday?" Emma cut her off. "Same time, same place?"

Nora tried to think of some possible reason why next Saturday wouldn't work, but she couldn't.

"And, Nora, I'm not going to tell you what snacks we're going to have, because I want them to be a surprise, but I found them on this online party snack website, and they're *amazing*."

"Great!" Nora said, trying to sound as much like Brody as possible. "Great!"

*

Nora worked on a Civil War battle report all afternoon. Every kid in the class had a battle to research. The Civil War had so many battles that nobody had to share.

Nora's battle wasn't really a battle. It was a siege, the Siege of Vicksburg, where General Ulysses S. Grant had surrounded Vicksburg for forty days until the city ran out of food and supplies and had to surrender.

That evening, Nora and her father ordered pizza for dinner. Her mother was dining with a visiting astronomer who had flown in for a conference.

"How's the class garden coming along?" Nora's father asked after a mouthful of pepperoni and mushrooms.

Nora felt herself bristling. Was he waiting for her to tell him he had been right that Mendel's peas would take too long to grow?

"I ended up planting radishes," Nora admitted. "The same as everybody else. I found a germination experiment to do on them, at least."

"That's my scientist girl."

Nora knew he meant the comment as a compliment, a way of letting her know he didn't think less of her for not turning out to be a younger version of Gregor Mendel. It wasn't her fault if peas took forever to grow. She wasn't to blame if monks had more time to wait around for a pea harvest than fourth graders did.

She tried to smile, but she felt a twinge of irritation. Why *couldn't* she grow plain, dumb radishes like everyone else? Why did she have to be constantly pushing back the frontiers of science?

"I probably won't prove anything new," Nora said.

"That's all right," her dad said. "Lots of scientists don't prove anything particularly *new.*"

"I probably won't prove *anything.*"

"Now, honey," her dad began, as she started picking the mushrooms off her slice of pizza and putting them in a pile on the edge of her plate, not that she had anything against mushrooms.

Nora cut him off. She couldn't bear parental encouragement right now.

"Did you ever want to be anything else but a scientist?" she asked.

Her father considered the question before he replied, the way he always did when she had asked him something important.

"I almost dropped my biochemistry major halfway through college," he said.

"You *did*?"

"Uh-huh. I was going to switch to history. Molecules were starting to seem awfully . . . I don't know . . . awfully *small*."

Her father's rueful smile made Nora laugh, even though she didn't want to.

"And then what happened?" she asked.

"I took a couple of history courses. And human beings started to seem awfully . . . big. The things they did were so . . . puzzling. I've never been able to make sense of the behavior of members of the species *Homo sapiens*. So I signed up again for biochemistry and never looked back. Though halfway through grading a stack of eighty exams, occasionally I have my doubts." He chuckled.

Then he went on, "Your mother almost became an English major. Your brother was pretty hardcore science all the way, but Sarah talked about dropping out of college to go backpacking through

Central America. Life can have twists and turns, and that's perfectly okay. You can end up someplace you never dreamed of going, and that's okay, too."

Nora was glad he had said that.

But in the end, she wasn't a twisty and turny kind of person.

In the United States, it is illegal to ship ant queens across state and even county lines, because new colonies of strange ants can damage ecosystems. That sounds like a good reason to me. But I still wish I could go online and buy one.

"I want to go up in a hot-air balloon," Brody told Nora and Mason on the Plainfield Elementary playground before school on Monday. "But my parents said it would cost too much."

Maybe Nora could get her parents to pay half, and she could go up in the balloon, too. Then she'd have her new thing accomplished, even if it would be the fifteenth new thing for Brody and the only new thing for her. It would be fascinating to fly so high, learning about hot and cold air currents, seeing things down below from a fresh perspective.

"How much does it cost?" Nora asked.

"Two hundred dollars," Brody told her.

Forget the hot-air balloon. Nora knew her parents would never pay a hundred dollars for that.

"Did you find your new thing?" she asked Mason. She hoped he hadn't. She didn't want to be the only one who couldn't find a single new thing to do. Then again, Amy hadn't done a new thing yet, either. She still had her heart set on a snake, and her mother was still saying no.

"Nope," Mason said. "Though . . . maybe talking about something new, thinking about something new, could count as a new thing? If you've never talked or thought about a new thing before?"

Nora shook her head.

"For me, at least?"

Nora shook her head again. "Not even for you."

Coach Joe led his team out to the class garden later that morning.

From a distance, the garden looked the same: fresh dirt newly plowed, with nothing growing yet. But when they got closer, Nora could see a faint line of green snaking across some of the rows.

The radishes were sprouting.

Some of Nora's radishes were sprouting: the control group that hadn't been frozen, baked, or nuked in the microwave. The others hadn't come up yet—maybe they would never come up?—except for a couple of tiny shoots.

That was interesting. Nora would have thought all the seeds that were baked, frozen, or nuked would respond the same way. What would make one tiny, teensy seed respond differently from another to the very same treatment?

"You did it!" Nora whispered to the brave few seeds that had made it. "Good for you!"

Then she caught herself.

Some of the lettuce seeds and other salad greens had started to sprout, too. Emma's pansies had yet to germinate.

"I'm going to *sing* to mine," Emma announced. "Maybe pansies are musical flowers that respond better to song."

In a clear, high soprano, Emma began singing, to the tune of "Row, Row, Row Your Boat": "Grow, grow, pansies, grow! Grow up very tall! Merrily, merrily, merrily, merrily, I love you best of all!"

Mason stared down at his radishes, which had sprouted the same as everyone else's.

"That's strange," he muttered.

Dunk's pumpkins hadn't done a thing: surprise, surprise. Nora knew from checking the seed catalog that pumpkins were supposed to be planted in late May or early June. Dunk scuffed at the dirt where his seeds were buried, as if to rouse them with a good, hard kick. A clod of earth flew up and hit Amy on the cheek.

"Dunk!" Coach Joe called. "Gardening is not a contact sport."

"Sorry," Dunk muttered.

Coach Joe explained to the class that as the shoots grew taller, the gardeners would have to thin their plants, uprooting some of them so the others would have more room to grow. Soon they'd have to start weeding their rows, too.

"Today we'll give them a good watering," Coach Joe said.

Dunk looked eagerly at the hose. Nora could tell he'd like to spray Emma so she'd squeal and giggle.

"Actually," Coach Joe said, looking Dunk's way, "*I'll* water them."

As the class stood back from the garden patch, Coach Joe sent a fine spray of water down each row to soak deep into the soil.

Seeds + sun + water + oxygen + nutrients in the soil = radishes.

Even though Nora knew it made scientific sense, right this minute it did seem like a miracle.

On Wednesday, Coach Joe's class wrote "persona" poems about the Civil War.

A persona poem was written from the point of view of a person who was someone other than you. The person in the poem could be the president of either side, like Abraham Lincoln or Jefferson Davis, or a general, like Grant or Robert E. Lee, or a common soldier, or a soldier's loved one back home. It didn't even have to be a *person*. It could be an animal or a bird, a flower or a flag, a musket or a cannon (Dunk brightened at that).

The point of a persona poem was to get inside the head of someone else (not that a cannon had a head) and see the world through that person's eyes (not that a cannon had eyes).

"I want you to think hard about your person," Coach Joe said. "When you try on someone else's identity, you might end up seeing something different from what you first supposed—completely different. That's the beauty and excitement of a persona poem."

So now Nora sat at her desk, trying to write a poem about the Civil War from the point of view of an ant.

Coach Joe had also told the class that the poem could be sort of like a riddle, where the reader might have to guess who was speaking: Was it a victorious general or a defeated one? A wounded soldier? A nurse? A horse who had ridden into battle? A butterfly with blood-stained wings?

Nora decided to make her readers read to the end of her poem to find out it was being told by an ant.

Though if they knew the poem was written by Nora, that might not be too hard to figure out.

What would an ant think about the Battle of Gettysburg, the bloodiest battle of the Civil War, which inspired President Abraham Lincoln to write his famous Gettysburg Address?

Nora picked up her pencil and started to write.

"July 3, 1863," she wrote at the top of her page, for her title.

Of course, an ant wouldn't know what day it was. Coach Joe had told them something in a poem that couldn't be true was called "poetic license." Nora didn't approve of poetic license. But it was hard to write a persona poem from the point of view of an ant without it. After all, an ant wouldn't think in words! And an ant wouldn't be writing a poem!

JULY 3, 1863

Feet stamp.
Feet tramp.
So many feet!
The walls of my tunnel collapse.
I dig and dig.
The walls fall in faster than I can dig them out.
Cannons boom.
Rifles fire.
So many guns!
My antennae hurt from sounds so loud.
My feet hurt from digging so hard.
This is a bad day
To be an ant.

Coach Joe had said they weren't going to share these poems in class; he needed to use the huddle for important announcements about the poetry unit. But Nora could hear KABOOMs coming across the room from the direction of Dunk's pod. His cannon persona poem sounded an awful lot like his pumpkin haiku.

As Coach Joe summoned the students back to his football-shaped rug, Nora noticed that Emma stayed at her desk, crying. Actual tears were running down Emma's face.

Why?

Emma silently handed Nora her own persona poem in response to Nora's questioning gaze.

NEWS FROM GETTYSBURG

My ma got the telegram today.
My pa is dead.

That was all Emma had written so far. Her poem was even shorter than a haiku. But Emma was crying as if her own mother had gotten the telegram and her own father had died on the battlefield.

"But—" Nora tried to think of something comforting to say. "It didn't really happen, Emma. Your father is completely fine!"

"It did happen!" Emma wailed. "Not to me, but to *somebody*. It did happen! Thousands of soldiers died at Gettysburg! One of them had to have had a daughter my age, and her mother got a telegram. It did happen to *someone*!"

Nora didn't know what to say next.

Emma was right.

But why would you cry about something that had happened so long ago? Why would you cry over a historical fact?

Yet as she watched Emma reach for a tissue and wipe her streaming eyes, her own eyes felt oddly damp around the corners.

My ma got the telegram today.

My pa is dead.

"Oh, Emma, don't cry." Nora awkwardly patted Emma's arm as Emma blew her nose. But now Nora was practically crying, too.

Coach Joe left his rocking chair in the huddle area and came over to see what was going on.

Nora handed him Emma's poem, and he read its two short lines.

Then he put one hand on Emma's shoulder and one on Nora's.

"This, my friends," he said, "is the power of poetry."

The Civil War was the deadliest war in American history. There were around 215,000 soldiers killed in action and 620,000 total dead (mainly from diseases like dysentery, typhoid fever, yellow fever, and malaria). For every single dead soldier, somebody could write a poem as sad as Emma's.

"I called this huddle," Coach Joe said, "to tell you the two big activities for the end of our poetry unit. First, we're going to have a class trip."

"Where can you go for a *poetry* trip?" Tamara asked.

That was a reasonable question. Nora had never heard of any nearby poetry museum. No famous dead poets had lived anywhere near Plainfield, so it couldn't be a class trip to a famous dead poet's house.

"We are going on a trip to *write* poetry," Coach Joe said.

"But we write poetry all the time in our pods," Mason pointed out.

"Ah," Coach Joe said, "but in the history of poetry, most poems have not been written by people sitting at school in pods."

That was almost certainly true.

"Many great poets, like William Wordsworth, wrote their poems outdoors in nature. Wordsworth wrote many of his while wandering around the mountains in the Lake District in England."

"Are we going to England?" Emma asked, excited now.

"No, Emma," he said. "That's a bit far and costly for us, I'm afraid."

Nora would enjoy a class trip writing poetry in the mountains near Plainfield. She could write a poem and scout for a new colony of ants at the same time.

"Other poets and writers," Coach Joe went on, "did their best work while sitting in cafés in Paris, sipping their cafés au lait and eating wonderful buttery rolls called croissants." He smacked his lips appreciatively.

"Are we going to *Paris*?" Emma asked, sounding even more excited.

Coach Joe grinned. "Not Paris, either. But we are going to a café. We'll walk to Café Rive Gauche—that's the name of the arty neighborhood of Paris. And we will drink *chocolat*—hot chocolate—and eat croissants. We'll take our poetry notebooks with us and sit there and write. I won't give you any prompts. I'll let you draw your inspiration from the trip itself."

"I don't want to eat a croissant," Nora heard Mason mutter to Brody.

"I've never had a croissant," Brody whispered back. "Another new thing for me!"

"What's the other big poetry activity?" Elise asked, as flushed with excitement about writing poetry in a café as Emma had been about going to England or France.

"We're going to have a special visitor to our class," Coach Joe replied. "A real poet. Well, all of you are also real poets now. A poet is someone who writes poetry. But our guest is a published poet, with several books of poetry to her credit. Her name is Molly Finger"—some kids laughed at the name—"and she'll tell us how she writes her poems, what her creative process is. And she'll read some of *your* poems, too, and give you some comments."

Nora wondered what Molly Finger would say about a bunch of ant poems. She'd probably tell Nora to find something more poetic than ants to write about. Butterflies, maybe. Or daffodils. Coach Joe had read the class a famous rhyming poem about daffodils. Nora remembered the last lines of it: "And then my heart with pleasure fills, and dances with the daffodils." She didn't think she could ever write a poem that good about ants.

That afternoon, it was a dog-walking, not a cat-cuddling, day at the animal shelter. Nora was surprised at how disappointed she felt to be out walking a rusty terrier named Tobster instead of petting a ginger cat named Cassidy.

"Do we have time to look at the cats?" she asked Amy's mother after she and Amy had each walked three dogs

"Sure," Mrs. Talia said. No mom was more will-ing to let kids hang out with animals than Amy's mom—unless the animal happened to be a snake.

Maybe Cassidy had already been adopted. For his sake, Nora hoped he was. Nobody—well, nobody who wasn't already a dedicated ant lover—could meet Cassidy and hold him on her lap for a whole half an hour without wanting to take him home to keep.

Nora's pulse quickened as she walked past the cages of meowing cats in the cat section of the shelter. She made herself go methodically, reading the name of each one, even though she knew Cassidy was either there or he wasn't, however quickly or slowly she looked for him.

Then, there he was: "Cassidy. Two years old. Loving and affectionate. Reason for adoptability: Elderly owner had to move into a pet-free care community."

Poor Cassidy!

He saw Nora and came to rub himself against the mesh side of his cage, meowing plaintively. Nora was sure he recognized her from the week before.

Cats could do that.

Unlike ants.

Nora stifled this disloyal thought. Ants were

ants. Cats were cats. It wasn't fair to blame ants for being ants any more than it was fair to praise cats for being cats.

"Do you want to hold him?" Amy's mother asked gently.

"She wants to *adopt* him," Amy said. "Right, Nora? You do want to adopt him, I know you do."

Five minutes later, Nora sat in the cat-human meeting room with Cassidy purring on her lap, even louder than he had the week before.

Ten minutes later, Amy's mom had called Nora's mom, who was done for the day at the university, and her mom was on her way to the shelter in her car.

Half an hour later, Nora was the owner of a cat carrier, a cat litter box, cat litter, cat bowls, scientifically approved cat food, half a dozen cat toys, a cat brush, a book on cat care, and a cat of her very own.

"Now, Nora," her mother said when they reached home. "You'll want to get Cassidy used to our house gradually. It takes a good while for cats to accustom themselves to new people and new places."

Nora barely listened as she lugged Cassidy's carrier, with Cassidy in it, up to her room and set it on her bed. Nora wasn't a *new* person to Cassidy. She was *his* person, the person he already loved, who had met him at the shelter not once but twice, each time as he purred louder than all the cats in the world put together.

"Go away," she told her mother, who stood hovering in the doorway. "I can handle it."

"All right," her mother said. "I'm downstairs if you need me."

Once the door was safely shut, Nora spoke softly to Cassidy, in her most soothing voice. "You're home now, Cassidy, and you're never going to have to live in a cage again. I'll take such good care of you, and I'll love you so much."

She hoped her ants weren't listening.

But she knew they weren't.

Drawing in her breath, Nora unlatched the carrier door and reached in for Cassidy.

With one swift motion of an angry paw, the cat swiped his claws against Nora's hand as he sprang from the carrier, leaped across her covers with a single bound, and darted under her bed.

"Cassidy!" Nora moaned, staring at her bleeding scratch.

She got down on the floor and peered into the dusty darkness beneath the bed, barely able to make out Cassidy's crouched form and glowing eyes.

"Cassidy!" Nora pleaded. "Come out! You're safe! This is your forever home, and I'm your forever owner!"

Cassidy didn't budge.

Nora tried more coaxing, to no avail.

She tried ignoring him. He was apparently glad to be ignored.

She abandoned him to go to dinner, hoping that when she returned he'd be there to greet her, past sulks forgotten. He wasn't.

At dinner, her mother had just said, "Well, these adjustments take time." She might as well have said, "I told you so."

All evening long, Nora waited for Cassidy to come out from under the bed. She set up his litter box in a corner of her room, to be moved downstairs to the mudroom when he was finally settled in as a member of the family—*if* that ever happened. She put food in his food bowl and water in his water bowl, hoping the smell of the food might draw him out. It didn't.

At bedtime, she checked on her ants, busy digging and tunneling as contentedly as could be. Well, the few ants that weren't dead.

Maybe she should have stuck with ants.

As she went downstairs to say good night to her parents, willing them not to ask her how things were going with Cassidy, the phone rang.

"I'll get it!" she announced, relieved at an excuse

not to have a long conversation. It was usually Amy calling for her, unless it was somebody trying to get her parents to give money for something.

It *was* Amy.

"What?" Nora asked. "I can't hear you. You have to speak louder."

"I can't," Amy said in a normal voice. Then she started whispering again, so softly Nora could barely make out the words.

"My mother doesn't know. . . . Oh, Nora, I did it!"

"Did what?" Nora asked, but she already knew.

"I found a snake!"

A cat can travel at a speed of approximately 30 miles (48 kilometers) per hour over a short distance. A cat can jump up to 6 times its height in a single bound. I think that is how fast Cassidy ran and how far Cassidy jumped to get away from me. ☹

10

Cassidy hadn't come out from under Nora's bed when Nora left for school Thursday morning. When she hurried home from school that afternoon, he was still in hiding. She couldn't tell if his food or water had been touched. His litter box still looked brand-new.

On Friday, he had eaten a few mouthfuls of the dry cat food in his bowl and had drunk a few sips of water, unless the water had evaporated into the air. There was one little wet spot in the cat box, and one small cat poop. That was something, but not enough to ease the hurt in Nora's heart.

On Saturday morning, when Nora came upstairs after breakfast, she froze in the doorway. Cassidy was on her unmade bed, curled into a ball. Had he finally realized this was Nora's house, *Nora*, the girl who had cuddled with him so lovingly at the shelter?

Barely breathing, Nora began inching her way into the room, so as not to startle him.

On the third inch, Cassidy leaped from her pillow and fled back under the bed.

Amy tried to console her on the phone.

"Cats aren't like dogs, Nora. Snookers was better than Mush Ball, but it took her a long while. And Mush Ball didn't come out from behind the couch for a long time!"

"How long?"

"I don't know. A whole day?"

It had been *three* days now for Cassidy.

As the hours slipped by, it was hard not to despair. The Confederate troops and residents of Vicksburg had held out against Grant's army for forty-seven whole days. What if Cassidy held out that long against Nora? Did Cassidy think of Nora as an invading army?

What if Cassidy held out against Nora forever?

At five-forty-five that afternoon, Nora stood by the front door of her house, her duffel packed with pj's, toothbrush, hairbrush, and clean clothes for tomorrow, waiting for her mother to find her car keys.

"Ready?" her mother asked, holding up her key ring.

Nora had never been less ready for anything in her whole life. With her luck, Cassidy was on the brink of coming out for a first tentative cuddle, and with Nora gone, he'd stalk back into hiding. Amy had told her how easy it is to hurt a cat's feelings, another way in which cats were different from ants.

"I guess so," she said, straining her ears upstairs for any faint meow and hearing none.

Once they reached Emma's house, Emma flung open the door before Nora even had time to ring the bell.

"*Bienvenue!*" Emma greeted her. "That's French for *welcome!* I'm learning a few words in French so I can talk in French when we go to write poetry at *le café.*"

Nora hardly heard what Emma was saying. For Emma was cradling her cat, Precious Cupcake, in the crook of her arm, and both Emma and Precious were wearing matching pink fluffy bathrobes.

Nora wanted to ask Emma how long it had taken Precious to get used to being Emma's cat, now a video star and bathrobe wearer, but she felt too jealous to admit how unsatisfactory her own cat was turning out to be.

"Don't worry," Emma said as Nora's eyes fastened on the embroidered letters on each robe that read EMMA'S SPA. "I have one for you, too!"

Five minutes later, Nora's duffel was stowed next to one of Emma's twin beds, which had a ruffled pink canopy stretched across the top of it. Over her pj's, Nora was wearing her own pink fluffy spa bathrobe.

"That's the theme of the sleepover!" Emma announced. "A night at the spa!"

Did sleepovers have themes? When Nora and Amy had sleepovers, they just talked, watched movies, and ate pizza.

"We're going to give ourselves facials!" Emma explained. "And try out new hairdos! And play that

nail polish game I told you about! And wait until you see the *snacks*!"

At least there was pizza first, eaten on normal plates at Emma's normal kitchen table, with her mother and older sister, to keep things from feeling too strange.

"I didn't do make-your-own pizzas," Emma said, "because I wanted to have lots and lots of time for the spa activities."

"I hope you're going to enjoy the spa experience," Mrs. Averill said as Nora nibbled on a piece of pepperoni pizza. "I told Emma I wasn't sure you were the spa type."

Well, Nora wasn't the spa type. But until this week, she hadn't been the cat-owning type, either.

If only Cassidy would decide he was the owned-by-Nora type. And decide it *soon.*

"I'm sure it will be lots of fun," Nora said. She was going to keep an open mind. A good scientist would keep an open mind in any new situation.

Emma fed Precious Cupcake some cheese from her slice of pizza. Nora would never feed Cassidy human food; it wasn't good for pets to have food meant for other species. But maybe Nora would never even have a chance to give Cassidy any treats at all.

"Okay!" Emma jumped up from the table as soon as Nora had swallowed the final bite of pizza. "To the spa!"

"Facials first!" Emma chirped.

Nora didn't know what a facial was, but she didn't ask. She'd find out soon enough.

"Step one, we wash our faces."

Emma led the way to the spacious bathroom that opened up off her bedroom. Nora had never known a kid who had a bathroom of her own.

"Where's the soap?" Nora asked, looking down at the sink.

Emma recoiled in horror. "We don't wash our faces with *soap*! Soap dries your skin out completely!"

Instead, Emma produced a bottle of cleansing lotion. Nora followed Emma's lead in applying it to her face and then wiping it off with the cloth provided.

"Now we open our pores!" Emma told her.

A few minutes later, Nora found herself sitting next to Emma, back at the kitchen table, a towel forming a tent over her head, leaning over a bowl of near-boiling water (Emma's mother helped with that part). The point was to let the steam rush up to her perspiring cheeks.

"Open our pores" apparently meant "sweat like a pig." Except that pigs had hardly any sweat glands, Nora remembered. Their inability to cool themselves off through perspiration was the chief reason they enjoyed wallowing in nice chilly mud.

"And now—the best part!"

From the fridge, Emma produced a bowl of some whitish, lumpy substance.

"Do we eat that?" Nora asked nervously.

Emma stared at her in disbelief. "No, silly! We put it on our faces!"

But—we just washed them!

Shaking her head in amusement, Emma led the way back to her bedroom, bowl in hand.

"Here," Emma instructed. "I'll show you how to do yours."

As Nora sat motionless on the edge of the guest bed, her hair tied back from her face, Emma rubbed the refrigerated mixture—"It's yogurt, Greek yogurt because that's the healthiest kind! And oatmeal, and honey"—onto Nora's forehead, cheeks, nose, and chin. It felt strange to have Emma's quick, deft fingers touching her face.

"Now you let it dry. Go ahead, lie down while I do mine."

Nora awkwardly laid herself flat on the bed.

"Oh, wait! I forgot the most important part!"

Emma darted downstairs and returned with another bowl of something Nora couldn't see.

"Close your eyes," Emma told Nora, as she had when fastening on the friendship bracelet, still on Nora's wrist.

Nora obeyed. Emma placed something cool and moist on Nora's shut eyelids.

"Cucumber slices!" Emma crowed.

"Um—why?"

"To reduce the puffiness around our eyes!"

Neither girl had any puffiness around her eyes whatsoever, as far as Nora could tell. But it was restful lying there, her head comfortable on Emma's pillow, the mask drying not unpleasantly onto her face, the cucumbers soothing against her eyes.

She could hear Emma humming happily as she applied the mask to her own face.

Then Emma screamed.

As only Emma could scream.

"Precious Cupcake, no! No! No!"

Nora jerked to an upright position, cucumber slices scattering onto the bedspread.

The cat had discovered the tempting bowl of yogurt, oatmeal, and honey. Her head was buried in it as she tried to lap up as much as she could.

"Oh, Precious, look at yourself! It's all over your face!"

Emma had snatched the cat away from the bowl and was holding her up, shaking her in despair. Now the cat and the girl had not only matching bathrobes but matching white masks on their faces as well.

"She wanted to get a facial, too," Nora said.

Emma started laughing first. Nora joined in. Both girls shrieked so loudly with giggles that Emma's older sister stuck her head in the room to see what was going on.

It was Emma's sister who handed Emma her phone to take the video.

It was Nora who held Precious Cupcake up in front of the phone as Emma filmed the video.

After the mask was scrubbed off Precious's face, all three girls watched the video of Precious Cupcake's first facial a dozen times, laughing as hard at the dozenth time as they had at the first.

So Nora had finally done a new thing she could tell Coach Joe. Adopting Cassidy didn't count and would never count unless Cassidy finally came out from under the bed, which might be never.

But Nora *had* co-starred in a cat video.

"This is the best sleepover ever!" Emma said.

But as the evening wore on, Nora started to feel more and more homesick. Maybe Cassidy, at this very moment, was looking around Nora's bedroom, wondering where that girl was who was going to be his new guardian and protector, the girl who right now was having her hair French-braided by Emma.

"You're lucky your hair is so long," Emma gushed. "Mine is too short for French braids, and it takes forever to grow. So, don't tell anyone, because it's supposed to be a surprise, but I'm going to get a completely new haircut!"

Instead of French-braiding her own hair, Emma fastened it with half a dozen butterfly barrettes, as if a flock of migrating butterflies had flown off course and landed on her head.

"Your hair is a great length," Emma said, cocking her head to one side as she studied Nora's new French-braided self. "But when it's not braided, it's soooo straight. Why don't I unbraid it and get my curling iron and give it a little wave?"

"Don't we need to play the nail polish game?" Nora asked.

If Nora had curls, she'd look like Emma's twin, except that her hair was longer and dark while Emma's was shorter and fair. Why would Emma want both of them to have curls? Wasn't the whole point of the sleepover for Emma to spend time with someone as different from herself as possible?

"The nail polish game!" Emma's face lit up. "Thanks for reminding me!"

Half an hour later, Nora had ten fingernails and ten toenails painted, each a different color, even though the game had turned out to be a failure;

you needed more than two people to play Spin the Nail Polish Bottle.

Emma had been shocked that Nora didn't know how to put on nail polish.

"But—but—but—" Emma had sputtered. "You can do all kinds of things with batteries, but you don't know how to put on *nail polish*?"

Now Nora did.

"We have to let it dry," Emma told her, "or it'll smudge. So let's play a sleepover game while we wait. I know! Let's play Truth or Dare!"

The name of the game made Nora nervous. She didn't want to have to tell Emma the truth about how bad she felt about being Emma's project. And she couldn't begin to imagine what kind of dares Emma had in mind.

"We ask each other questions," Emma explained, waving her hands around with outstretched fingers to create a drying breeze. "And we have to give a true answer. No lies! And if we don't want to tell the truth because it's too embarrassing, then we have to do whatever dare the other person says. Only it can't be anything dangerous, of course. So who should go first?"

Cats sleep 16 to 18 hours a day. That means cats sleep two-thirds of their lives away. If you poke a cat's tail while it is sleeping, the tail will twitch. But you can't poke your cat's tail if your cat is sleeping under your bed.

Nora didn't want to go first.

She didn't want to go second, either.

What she really wanted was to go home and see if Cassidy had finally decided to lie on her bed and do the things a cat was supposed to do. It was too sad to be giggling over somebody else's cat videos when her own cat was such a sad disappointment.

"Okay, I'll start," Emma said. "Here's my first question for you. Who do you have a crush on?"

Nora felt a sweet surge of relief. That one wasn't embarrassing or scary.

"Nobody."

"Come on, Nora. Is it Mason? Is it Brody? Everybody has a crush on somebody."

"I don't."

Emma sighed, but she seemed to accept, grudgingly, that what Nora had said was true. After all, wasn't Emma expecting Nora to give answers completely opposite from what Emma would have given? Wasn't that the whole point of the newness-challenge sleepover?

"Okay, you ask me a question," Emma instructed.

All Nora could think of was to turn Emma's same question back at her. She hoped that copying other people's questions was allowed.

"Who do *you* have a crush on?" Nora asked.

Emma blushed. "Promise you won't tell anyone. Even Amy. Promise!"

Nora promised.

"I sort of have a crush on . . . Dunk."

As if that hadn't been totally obvious to the entire fourth grade for months, given that Emma giggled whenever Dunk burped, belched, or made rude noises with his hand under his armpit.

"Okay," Emma said, "here's another one for you.

What's the most embarrassing thing that ever happened to you at the mall?"

Was the most embarrassing thing having to say she never went to the mall?

"Nothing," Nora admitted. "I mean, I never go to the mall."

Emma's eyes widened. Even though it should have been Nora's turn to ask a question, Emma kept on going. "What's the dumbest TV show you secretly like to watch?"

"My family doesn't have a TV," Nora confessed.

Emma paused, as if trying to come up with a question for which Nora could finally give a satisfying answer. "What do you like *best* about me, and what do you like *least*?"

Until this moment, Nora could have come up with a lot of things she liked about Emma. Right now, tired, nervous, and worried about Cassidy, she couldn't think of anything. She certainly didn't like that Emma was making her play this awful game at a sleepover that was happening only because Emma had decided to use her for a prize-winning project for school.

"Give me a dare instead," Nora said miserably.

Emma tossed her butterfly-studded curls. "Okay then. I dare you to do a funny dance to my favorite song, 'Kitten Love.'"

Emma grabbed her phone and touched the screen, and the song began to play: peppy, bouncy music about someone who was in love with her cat. A cat, presumably, that came out from under the bed occasionally and purred on the person's lap.

Nora was good at playing basketball and softball. She was terrible at dancing.

Feeling the heat rise to her face, Nora struggled to her feet and tried out a couple of awkward steps with her feet, clawing the air with her hands as if they were paws.

Emma burst out laughing.

This was too much. It was all too much. Nora hadn't come to Emma's house to be laughed at. Maybe Emma would call Bethy in California tomorrow and tell her how ridiculous Nora had looked doing the dance, and they'd both laugh at Nora together.

Nora stopped dancing. "Oh, hey, I just remembered something."

"What?"

"I have to go home. *Now.* I forgot to feed my ants. The song reminded me. Cats—pets—ants—hungry—feed—go home."

Maybe Emma would understand her homesickness more if Nora told her about Cassidy: how much she wanted to have her own cat to cuddle, and how heartbroken she was that Cassidy had turned out to be the least cuddly cat in the universe.

"I'm sorry," Nora added. "It's been a very nice party." Well, some parts of it had been nice, and lots more fun than Nora had expected. "But I really do have to go."

Nora expected Emma to fly into a rage, but instead Emma's lips trembled and her eyes glistened, as if she might cry.

What on earth was going on here?

"We didn't even have the snacks," Emma whispered.

Was *that* why Emma was about to burst into tears? Or was she just sad that her newness project was spoiled?

"We can still have them," Nora said. Even though Emma had made fun of her humiliating dance,

Nora could still be polite to Emma. "It will take my mom a few minutes to come and get me. Can I use your phone to call her?"

Silently, Emma handed her phone to Nora. It was awful to make the call with Emma standing right there, as Nora told her mother she needed to come home right now to feed her ants. All her mother said was, "Oh, honey. Okay, I'll be there soon."

Emma led the way downstairs to the dining room table, where the snacks were laid out in their full splendor.

Colored marshmallows, with an unwrapped Tootsie Roll stuck in the top of each one.

"Like nail polish bottles. See?" Emma said flatly.

Tiny sandwiches made of bread cut in the shape of flip-flops, with the straps made of strips of green onion fastened with itty-bitty cherry tomatoes.

"Like you'd put on your feet after a pedicure," Emma explained, "so the nail polish doesn't smudge."

Pink-frosted, heart-shaped cookies.

"Those aren't a spa thing," Emma said. "They're more of a friendship thing. . . ." Her voice trailed off.

Nora heard her mother's car pulling into the driveway. She remembered to take off the embroidered spa bathrobe and drape it over a dining room chair, but she'd have to dash outside in her pajamas.

"Thanks, Emma," Nora managed to say, over the sudden lump in her throat. "I'm . . . sorry."

And she was. Even though Emma was the one who should be even sorrier.

Nora fled to the car, grateful that her mother would know the answer without having to ask the question.

How could Nora have failed at every single new thing she had thought of trying?

She wasn't being a young Mendel for the twenty-first century, or proving anything new about dumb radishes.

She wasn't tackling a new sport, or even a new position in the same sport.

Anybody with ears would be grateful she wasn't playing a new instrument.

She wasn't going up in a hot-air balloon.

She didn't have a new pet, not really. Having Cassidy under her bed was no different from having no cat, except that her heart hadn't ached before, and it did now.

She had tried so hard to have fun doing the new things at the sleepover, from getting the facial to polishing her nails to making the cat video. But then Emma had acted disappointed in her for not having the right answers to the Truth or Dare questions, and had laughed at her—laughed right to her face—when Nora had done her best to do the crazy dance.

So in the end she had nothing new to show for herself. Nothing, nothing, nothing.

A cat's hearing is better than a dog's. A cat can hear sounds up to 2 octaves higher than a human can and 1 octave higher than a dog can. Cats have more than 100 different vocal sounds. Dogs have only 10. But I wish my cat would love me the way Mason and Brody's dog loves them.

Amy's small green snake lay curled on soft grass in the bottom of its glass terrarium, beneath a makeshift lid weighted down with two rocks.

"I couldn't find the real lid," Amy explained to Nora on Sunday afternoon. "The terrarium was in the garage, but the lid wasn't with it, so I used this piece of glass instead."

"Your mother still doesn't know about him—or her?"

"My mom hates coming in my room," Amy said.

Nora didn't like Amy's room much herself, but

she was used to it now. Dirty clothes covered Amy's bed. "They're not that dirty," Amy had told her. "I might wear them again. You can wear pants or sweaters several times, you know." Leashes, water bowls, and books on pet care were everywhere underfoot. Amy's desk was heaped high with school announcements crumpled from her backpack, interesting rocks she had picked up on walks, and seashells from a family vacation to Florida.

"I don't know if Fred is a boy or a girl. It's hard to tell," Amy said.

"Do you take Fred out sometimes?" Nora asked.

"I try to, but so far it hasn't worked. I think Fred misses life in the world. The last time I took her—him—out, she—he—wriggled away and slipped under the bed, and you wouldn't believe how long it took me to find him—her."

So far, Fred sounded like Cassidy.

"I guess I should set Fred free," Amy said sadly. "How long do we have to do the new thing for? Did Coach Joe say?"

Nora tried to remember. "I think he said a month. It probably depends on what the new thing is."

Amy considered Nora's comment.

"If the new thing is a pet," Amy said, "I think

you need to have the pet long enough to form a relationship. Fred and I haven't bonded yet. Have we, Fred?"

She leaned over the terrarium. Fred made no response.

Amy hadn't bonded with Fred any more than Nora had bonded with Cassidy. If Amy was going to set Fred free, did that mean Nora should take Cassidy back to the shelter? Cassidy had certainly seemed happier there than living with Nora.

"Oh!" Amy said. "I almost forgot! How was your sleepover with Emma?"

For some reason, Nora didn't want to tell even Amy the truth. Her hair was unbraided now, her nails scrubbed clean of polish with plenty of rubbing alcohol, which had taken forever (nobody in Nora's house owned any nail polish remover). She had tried her best to forget all about it.

But she couldn't forget Emma's pale, strained face as she had shown Nora the platters of uneaten spa snacks. And the tears in Emma's eyes when Nora had said goodbye.

"It was okay," Nora said. "But I don't think we'll be having another one any time soon."

Emma's newness project was a total failure, too.

Emma caused a sensation by arriving at the Plainfield Elementary School playground on Monday morning wearing brightly patterned, flowing, pantaloon-style pants, topped with a scarlet vest. On her head, she wore a turban.

"This is my Arabian Nights look!" Nora heard Emma telling Elise and Tamara. "What do you think?"

Emma twirled in place, ankle bells tinkling faintly.

She was avoiding looking in Nora's direction, unless Nora was imagining it.

"What is *that*?" Amy whispered to Nora.

Nora shrugged. Something about Emma's new style had her worried.

The other girls seemed clearly impressed.

"Ooh!" Elise gushed.

"I want a turban like yours!" Tamara cried.

"Maybe *your* new thing could be a turban," Brody said to Mason.

"Or maybe not," Mason replied.

Even Coach Joe, once the morning bell had

rung, couldn't refrain from commenting. When the class assembled for their morning huddle, he called Emma "Scheherazade," and explained that Scheherazade was a famous storyteller who had kept a Persian sultan—or king—mesmerized with her stories for 1,001 nights.

The poetry prompt for the day, Coach Joe told the class, was "I remember . . ."

That was all. The idea was to write a list of things you remembered, with a few interesting details, starting each line with the same words: "I remember . . ."

Right now Nora didn't like any of her memories.

But Coach Joe had said sometimes bad memories can make the best poems.

So she started writing.

I remember when my ants were all alive instead of
  mostly dead.
I remember when Cassidy purred on my lap at the
  shelter, so soft and so warm.
I remember how Cassidy hasn't purred on my lap
  even once since he came home with me.
I remember how Emma and I used to be friends,
  instead of this weird thing we are now.

I remember when Emma and I laughed so hard at
Precious Cupcake's facial.
I remember how Emma looked when I left the
party early, like she was ready to cry.
I remember when I wasn't even trying to do
anything new.
I remember when I didn't know yet how hard new
was going to be.

Outside in the class garden, the radishes and lettuce were growing into little plants. Emma's pansies had poked up, too. Emma claimed it was
because she had sung so many songs to them to
encourage them to push their way up through the
dirt.

Dunk's pumpkins hadn't sprouted. But Dunk
didn't seem worried.

"Wait till they do!" he said to everyone around
him. "Then your radishes will be sorry!"

It was the day for thinning the plants, pulling
up every other one so each remaining plant would
have more room to grow.

Nora looked at her short row of non-baked, nonfrozen, non-microwaved radishes. It seemed so sad to pull up half of them, after she had already destroyed three-quarters of the original seeds with her scientific experiments.

Instead, she decided to transplant the ones she would have thrown away, moving them over into the section of her row where the experimented-upon seeds would have sprouted.

It was slow work. The plants were so small! It was hard to dig up each one, with its tiny roots, get it settled into fresh dirt, and pat the dirt into place around it.

Nora looked up from her toil to see Dunk watching her.

"What are *you* doing?" he asked.

He sounded genuinely curious, so Nora answered honestly.

"I'm giving them a chance to live," she said.

"They better do their living fast before my pumpkins come," Dunk said, but he reached down and righted one of her radishes that had tipped over.

That was a surprise.

Nora realized she didn't know what Dunk's new thing was going to be. He hadn't talked about it, unlike the way a lot of kids—well, mainly Brody—were doing.

But as far as Nora was concerned, being kind to a radish plant counted.

"No, Dunk!" Emma said as Dunk turned around in the cafeteria line at lunch to give a playful tug on her turban.

Standing behind Emma, Nora heard panic in Emma's voice. This wasn't Emma's usual giggling no. Emma meant it this time.

Nora knew this.

Dunk didn't.

"What's under there?" he taunted, with the big, happy grin he wore when teasing Emma. "Did you grow horns?"

Thomas, the silent boy in Nora and Emma's pod, had fallen into line behind Nora.

"What do you want to bet Emma grew horns?" Dunk called over to him.

Of course, Thomas said nothing. He didn't even bother to answer Dunk's question with a shrug.

"Or lice!" Dunk chortled. "Thomas, what do you

want to bet Emma has lice, and she got her whole head shaved off, and she's bald now?"

Dunk didn't even wait for Thomas not to answer. Tucking his still-empty tray under his arm, he made another snatch at Emma's turban as Emma was picking up her own tray.

"Stop it!" Emma shouted, with no hint of a giggle. "Dunk, I told you to stop!" Her tray clattered to the floor as she clapped both hands over her head.

Dunk set his tray down on the rails in front of the serving station and gave one last two-fisted yank at Emma's turban.

It came off in his hand.

Emma *was* bald.

Black is the most common hair color in the world. The rarest is red, found in just 1 percent of the population; next most rare is blond hair, like Emma's. Hair is the fastest-growing tissue in the human body, except for bone marrow. On average, hair grows 6 inches, or about 15 centimeters, each year. The average person has 100,000 to 150,000 strands of hair on his or her head. We shed somewhere around 50 to 150 strands of hair a day. When a hair falls out, it will usually regrow. I hope Emma's hair regrows soon.

13

No, Nora saw, not completely bald, but Emma's hair was as short as a boy's, sticking up in trampled spikes like the stubble of harvested corn in an autumn field.

Emma shrieked.

And shrieked.

And shrieked.

Instantly, one of the lunch ladies descended upon Dunk, wrenched Emma's turban from his hands, and plopped it back onto Emma's head.

Nora stared, appalled.

Even Dunk was too shocked at what he had done to utter another word. He flushed brick red with shame, as if somehow his prank had caused this terrible thing to happen to Emma's head.

"Your hair . . . ," Nora whispered, before she could stop herself. "What happened to your hair?"

Emma whirled around to face Nora, her pale face dotted with two flaming spots of fury, one on each cheek. "It's *your* fault!" Emma accused Nora.

"What? How?"

All Nora could think of was the butterfly barrettes from the spa hair salon. Had Emma's hair somehow come off when she removed them?

"Did it . . . happen at the sleepover?"

"No!" Emma almost shrieked. "What happened at the sleepover was a big fat nothing! I tried so hard to be a good friend, Nora! I made you a friendship bracelet, and I invited you to a sleepover, and came up with the best theme for a sleepover *ever*, with the *best* activities, and the *best* snacks. And then you didn't like any of it—don't say you did, because you didn't. You left early with a lame excuse, but I knew you just couldn't stand being there with me anymore!"

"But—" Nora tried to protest, but Emma cut her off.

"I was so depressed the next day that I decided to cheer myself up and finally do my new thing, do the newest new thing of anybody in our class, and get an extra-new hairstyle. My regular stylist wasn't there that day, but I decided to go through with it anyway, so I told the other stylist I wanted a pixie cut, and I guess she was an extra-new stylist, or at least she was an extra-terrible stylist, because *this* is what she thought a pixie cut was. *This!*"

Nora was definitely sorry about Emma's disastrous haircut. But it wasn't Nora's fault, it wasn't!

"I tried to like the party," Nora said.

"You *tried* to like the party," Emma shot back.

"I *did* like it! I liked lots of it!"

But all I could think about was how your cat loves you so much and my cat doesn't love me at all. And how you kept acting like we were friends, when all the time I was just your project for school!

Emma wasn't even listening. "You wouldn't even say what you liked best and liked least about me.

Because you don't like anything best about me, do you? You like everything *least* about me. Don't you, Nora? Go ahead and tell me what you like least about me. Just say it!"

Nora had been pushed far enough. So Emma really wanted to know what Nora liked least about her? All right, Nora would tell her.

"*Here's* what I like least about you. You're silly, and unscientific, and you have to be the queen all the time, and make everyone do what *you* want, and if they don't, you rush off and get your hair chopped off and then you have the nerve to blame *them*!"

Emma's eyes filled with tears. "Here's what I like least about *you*. You're like a *machine*, a science machine. You may know everything about science, but when it comes to people, you don't know anything. You should live in a world with nothing but *ants*. And even your *ants* probably don't like you!"

"Girls! Girls!" the lunch lady said. "You're holding up the line. If you're going to call each other names, get your food and do it at your table!"

Stunned, Nora accepted whatever the lunch lady dumped on her tray and stumbled over to a table on the far side of the cafeteria, as far away from Emma's table as she could find.

It wasn't true that nobody liked her.

Amy liked her.

Brody liked her.

Even Mason, who hardly liked anything or anybody, liked her.

Tamara and Elise liked her, though probably not as much as they liked Emma.

Her ants *would* have liked her, if liking people was something ants did.

Maybe Cassidy would like her someday. He used to like her, before she had taken him home to be her forever cat.

So why did she feel like putting her head down on the table to cry?

"What was *that* about?" Amy asked Nora at lunch recess. She had found Nora on one of the playground swings, not swinging, just sitting, her feet scuffing the ground.

"Emma hates me," Nora whispered.

"Well . . . ," Amy said. "She shouldn't have made

you her newness project. That was a crummy thing to do."

Nora reflected for a moment.

Maybe . . . maybe Emma *had* just wanted them to be closer, better friends? But why now, in the very month Coach Joe had challenged his class to do something new?

Yet . . . Emma had sent her a sympathy card the last time all her ants had died.

Emma thought Nora's niece, Nellie, was adorable. She had organized a whole party so the other girls could come over and admire Nellie.

Forced by Coach Joe to work together, Nora and Emma had won a prize at the science fair. Nora could still hardly believe that had happened.

Nora and Emma had even had fun making the video of Precious Cupcake's facial.

"Are you going to take off her friendship bracelet now?" Amy asked.

Nora looked down at the faded strings knotted onto her wrist. She gave a tug at the bracelet, wondering if the last threads would snap. They didn't. "I'll cut it off tonight, with scissors."

At home that evening, after a whole afternoon of

cold silence from Emma in their pod, Nora found a pair of scissors and got ready to snip the bracelet off her wrist.

But then . . . she didn't.

Instead, she sat by her ant farm, where the last two ants lay dead now, with no other ants left to bury them, and cried the tears she hadn't let herself cry at school.

As she wiped her eyes, she felt something brush against her bare leg.

Something like a cat.

Exactly like a cat.

Nora didn't let herself breathe, or utter a single word. She gave her lap one gentle pat of invitation.

Cassidy looked at her. She looked back.

Avoiding any abrupt motions, Nora pulled the afghan from the bottom of her bed and spread it over her lap to make it more soft and alluring.

Then Cassidy jumped up onto the bed and crept onto her lap, kneading the afghan with his front paws before settling into place. Nora wasn't sure if he would allow her to pet him or not. She ran her hand timidly over his ginger fur.

He started purring.

He kept on purring. And purring. And purring. And purring. And purring.

And then he purred some more.

Kittens learn how to purr when they are a couple of days old. While purring, domestic cats produce 25 to 150 vibrations per second. Big wild cats that do not roar, such as mountain lions, can purr. But my cat purrs the best.

As Coach Joe's team of poets walked to the Café
Rive Gauche on Friday morning, Emma led the
way. A French beret, tilted at a becoming angle,
covered the cropped curls. She was dressed all in
black: slim black pants, silky black top.

"French women wear black because black is so
sophisticated," Nora had overheard Emma telling Tamara as the class had lined up for the ten-
block walk from school to downtown. Emma and
Nora hadn't spoken a word to each other since
their quarrel on Monday. At least Cassidy now

slept curled in the crook of Nora's legs every single night.

Amy was telling Nora that Fred-the-snake had escaped again. "Even though I had two rocks holding the lid in place! And I can't find him—her—anywhere! And if my mom finds her—him—first, she's going to kill me!"

Mason carried a plastic bag containing three Fig Newtons, since he had no intention of trying croissants.

Brody's face glowed with poetic inspiration. He wore a tie-dyed T-shirt and a big peace sign on a chain around his neck. Coach Joe had told the class that poets had written poems in cafés not only in Paris, but also in San Francisco during the 1950s and 1960s. This was Brody's try at a 1960s hippie look.

Dunk swaggered along, kicking a can he had found in the gutter. "Pow! Kaboom!" He looked over at Nora as he did it, as if he was kabooming her instead of the can. It was clear he blamed her for the shock he had gotten when he pulled off Emma's turban, and for Emma's frosty silence ever since.

The other customers at the Café Rive Gauche looked up from their lattes and laptops, visibly startled, as Coach Joe led the class into the café.

"Don't mind us," Coach Joe told them with a grin. "We're here to write poetry."

This answer didn't appear reassuring. Evidently the other coffee drinkers had never seen so many poets crowded into one space.

It took a long time to order all the croissants and *chocolat,* even though Coach Joe had alerted the café so extra baristas would be ready to assist. When Nora and Amy finally had their food—apricot-almond croissant for Nora, chocolate croissant for Amy—they found a table for two outside in the café courtyard, under the shade of a large tree in new leaf.

"My poem is going to be called 'Eek! My Snake Escaped!'" Amy said.

"Good title!" Nora agreed.

She didn't know what her own poem would be. All she could think about was her fight with Emma.

Had she been wrong about Emma?

Or had Emma been wrong about her?

Or had they both been wrong about each other?
She started writing.

> Sometimes it's hard
> To know what's true and what isn't.
> Sometimes it's hard
> To know who's right and who's wrong.
> Sometimes it might not even matter
> When all you want is to be someone's friend again.

It looked short on the page, but Nora couldn't think of anything else she wanted to add. How could she be done with her poem already, when she hadn't even had the first bite of croissant?

Well, Coach Joe had told the class that a poem was whatever length it was. A poem took however much time it took.

Dunk and Emma headed outside, too, Dunk with four croissants on his tray. Emma must have forgiven him for the turban yanking, because when he said something to her, she giggled as in days of yore.

"Oh, Dunk!" Nora heard Emma say. Her own pencil rested motionless as Amy's pencil raced across the page.

Dunk said something else to Emma.

Nora was almost sure she heard her own name.

She waited for Emma to giggle again. Maybe Emma and Dunk were laughing together at the girl who loved only (dead) ants. Emma didn't even know that now Nora had a cat of her own, a cat who finally loved her back.

But the next words Nora heard were, "No, Dunk! You can't!"

Dunk muttered something else.

"It's too mean!" Emma said, sounding almost as upset as she had in the cafeteria line on Monday.

What was too mean? Nora was sure she heard her own name again.

". . . never going to speak to you again! And this time I mean it!"

Emma flounced away from Dunk, the same two spots of fury reddening her cheeks.

"Wait, Emma!" Dunk called after her.

Emma didn't look back. She plunked herself down with Tamara and Elise at the table next to Nora and Amy's. As if nothing had happened, she started telling them about the ode she was going to write to Precious Cupcake. She had already found the best rhymes for it.

"You can go to the computer and google *rhyme* and the word you want to find some rhymes for, and they come right up! There are heaps and heaps for *Cupcake*, well, for *cake*, but I found rhymes—well, they sort of rhyme—for *Precious*, too! *Dresses!* 'Precious loves to wear dresses!' And she does! Or *freshest!* 'Of all cats, Precious is the freshest!'"

Dunk stood rooted where Emma had left him, clutching his croissant-laden tray. What could Dunk have said to Emma that would make her react that way? And what did it have to do with Nora?

Coach Joe's students wrote for another half an hour—Nora left her poem the way she first wrote it—and then it was time to walk back up the hill to Plainfield Elementary.

The other café customers didn't look disappointed to see them go.

Emma snubbed Dunk for the rest of the day. It would have been hardly noticeable, given that Emma had already been snubbing Dunk—and Nora—all week. But there was a new lift to Emma's chin and a new glint in her eyes.

Something was definitely going on.

And it definitely had to do with Nora.

"Emma?" Nora asked her, as the rest of the class was gathering for the afternoon Civil War huddle.

"What?" Emma snapped.

"Is everything . . . okay?"

Emma stared at Nora, as if a question like that, from someone as supposedly smart as Nora, was too dumb to believe.

"Oh, yes!" Emma said. "Everything is totally terrific!"

When the dismissal bell rang for the day, Nora heard Emma say to Dunk, "Remember what I said!" And she heard Dunk say to Emma, "Maybe I will, and maybe I won't!"

Emma turned on her heel and stalked away, heading not toward Tamara and Elise—"See you later!" she called after them—but toward the class garden. Nora followed at a safe distance, not to be seen.

In the garden, Emma stood motionless as a scarecrow. The thought of a scarecrow made Nora feel guilty again for Emma's botched haircut, though Emma's spiky wisps of hair were hidden under her

French poet's beret. And the haircut *hadn't* been Nora's fault, no matter how much Emma tried to pretend it was.

Scientists are curious people, and Nora was nothing if not a scientist.

She drew closer.

Emma wasn't singing to her pansies.

She was standing guard over Nora's radishes.

Nora approached. What did she have to lose? Emma already hated her.

Emma looked over at her, startled.

"What were you and Dunk fighting about at the café?" Nora asked. She might as well ask the question and be done with it.

"It's none of your business!" Emma said, but her darting eyes said otherwise.

"I heard you say my name."

Emma hesitated. "Dunk said . . . Dunk said . . . he was going to pour vinegar on your radishes."

Nora knew the acid in vinegar would kill plants. She was surprised Dunk had paid enough attention to plant science to know that, too. But right now that wasn't what surprised her most.

"Why me? What did I ever do to Dunk?"

As soon as she asked the question, Nora knew the answer: Dunk was going to kill her radishes to get even with her for making Emma sad enough to yell in the cafeteria with big tears in her eyes.

Little had Coach Joe known what could happen when he set his class the challenge of doing something new.

Nora had answered the first question herself, but now she had a second one.

"But—why do *you* care?"

"I just do." Emma's voice trembled. "Most of your radishes died, and you had only these ones left. I saw you transplanting them—and you *were* talking to them while you did it! I heard you explaining to them what you were doing and why. So I thought, you love your radishes the way I love my pansies, and even though you hate me, I don't hate you, and I don't want your radishes to die."

"I don't hate you," Nora said over the huge, choking lump in her throat. "I've never hated you. I just felt bad being your project."

"Being my what?"

"Your newness project. For Coach Joe's challenge."

Emma stared at her. "What are you talking about?"

"You know, how he said to spend time with someone as different as possible from you? So you picked me?"

Emma's mouth dropped open. "How could you—Nora, how could you have thought *that*? You weren't my new thing! My new thing was always going to be a new haircut. I even told you about it at the sleepover, remember? I was saving it for a big surprise on the day of the newness festival, so I could win the newness prize, but I was so sad last weekend that I went and did it sooner. And then, well, I didn't expect it would turn out to be *this* new."

"But . . . you invited me for the sleepover right after Coach Joe had the newness huddle. Like, ten minutes after!"

"I was thinking about Bethy. And how she had moved away. And how she and I used to have sleepovers all the time. And how you and I had never had a sleepover. And how we totally should! We had so much fun doing our science fair project together, you know we did. And I love your niece Nellie so much."

Nora tried to process these new thoughts. Could she really have been so wrong about everything? And not only wrong, but unscientific, to jump to a conclusion without sifting through all the evidence?

"We're total opposites," Nora said. "So I just thought—"

"True friends can be opposites," Emma said. "Look at Mason and Brody."

Nora was still confused. "At the sleepover, you laughed at me when I did the dance!"

"It was *supposed* to be a funny dance. That was the whole dare: to do a funny dance. I laughed because I thought it was funny!"

"But . . . I'm not the type to do a funny dance."

Though she wasn't sure anymore that people came in types, the way ants or radishes did.

"What was really funny," Nora remembered, feeling her mouth curve up into a smile, "was how Precious Cupcake looked with the mask on for her facial."

Emma burst out laughing. "Wait." She pulled out her phone. "Let's watch the video again."

Standing in the garden by Nora's radishes and

Emma's pansies, they played the video of Nora holding up the cat to show off her new spa look, both girls giggling as hard as they had at the party.

"Anyway," Emma said, "the whole point of Coach Joe's assignment was to do things we're *not* the type of people to do."

"I have a cat now," Nora blurted out. "I got a cat last week from the animal shelter."

Emma stared at her for an unbelieving moment, and then she gave a squealing shriek of joy. "You do? You have a cat? What kind? Is it a girl or a boy? What's its name? Do you have any videos? Why didn't you *tell* me?"

"It's a boy cat," Nora said. "His name is Cassidy. I don't have any videos. Well, not yet. I should have told you about him at the sleepover, but I was so sad he wouldn't come out from under my bed, or do anything with me, so I thought maybe I was going to have to take him back to the shelter. He didn't come out for days and days!"

Emma gave another squealing shriek. "Precious Cupcake was the same way! The exact same way! I was sure she hated me! And look at how she is now!"

Nora felt like crying with happy relief.

"You know," Emma said then. "The spa snacks? I was too sad to eat them, so my mom put them in the freezer to save for later. I was thinking . . . if you'd like . . ."

"I'd love to," Nora said.

Emma and I are not the only people who think cat videos are funny. Some cat videos on YouTube have been seen more than 100 million times.

Nora had never been to a festival of newness before. No one else in their class had, either. Maybe this was a new thing for the entire world.

"I've never done anything like this with a class," Coach Joe announced on the day of the newness celebration, held on a Friday afternoon in late May. "My new thing as a teacher has been encouraging you to try new things as my students."

Parents had not been invited. But Emma's mother, as their PTA room parent, had provided balloons with the word NEW on them, and mini-cupcakes from a new bakery in town. On the party table was also a huge bowl of salad tossed from lettuce and radishes harvested from the class garden. A bouquet of Emma's Ocean Breeze pansies sat in a glass jar, the pansy faces seeming to smile on the proceedings.

The only outside guest was the poet Molly Finger, who had told Coach Joe she wouldn't miss a newness festival for anything.

Nora couldn't decide if Molly Finger looked like a poet or not. She wasn't sure what a poet was supposed to look like. Molly Finger was older than Nora's parents, but a poet could be any age. She was stouter than Nora's parents, but a poet could be any shape. She had crinkly gray hair framing a smiling face. She didn't look poetic, exactly, but when she read the class some of her poems, she sounded exactly like a real poet would sound.

After her reading, Poet Molly went from pod to pod to look at students' poetry and make suggestions. Nora wished they could skip that part. She loved showing her science fair projects to the judges, but she felt shy sharing her poems with a published poet. But she could overhear snatches of

Molly's comments, and none of them were mean. She even praised Dunk's pumpkin and cannon poems for their "explosive energy."

When she finally arrived at Nora's pod, she laughed at Mason's funny negative haiku ("Very clever!"), picked out some good details in Thomas's persona poem about Robert E. Lee, and told Emma her cat sounded adorable. (It wasn't exactly a compliment about Emma's *poem*, but Emma beamed anyway.)

"My poems are strange," Nora apologized to Molly in advance as she handed over her stack of ant poems. "They're about something most people wouldn't think is very poetic."

"A poem can be about anything," Molly reassured her.

"Well, these are . . . well, they're about ants."

The poet read through Nora's poems once. Then she read through them again.

"You have a real gift for observation," Molly told Nora. "And a gift for making others see what you love through your loving eyes. You might consider writing a few more ant poems and making them into a chapbook."

Nora guessed a "chapbook" was a little book of poems.

"Really?" Nora asked her, disbelieving.

"Really," Molly Finger said, with another of her wide smiles.

That was an amazing thought right there: Nora as the author of an entire book of poems.

"All right," Coach Joe said when Molly had finished her rounds. "Now it's time to do our sharing.

I have everyone's name in this baseball mitt. I'll pick the first name, and then each one of you will draw the name of the next person."

Nora squeezed Emma's hand.

Emma squeezed back.

Coach Joe reached into the mitt. "Thomas, you're up to bat first."

"I gave a talk about my pet lizard at my church," said the boy who never spoke in class.

Even his saying that much caused a ripple of surprise in Coach Joe's room. Thomas played a short clip of his talk on the big screen in the front of the classroom. He didn't sound shy or awkward; he sounded like a kid who talked all the time.

"So how did you like giving the talk?" Coach Joe asked Thomas.

Thomas shrugged.

"Do you think you'll give more talks?"

Thomas shook his head no.

The next kid had eaten at an Ethiopian restaurant, where diners scooped their food with pieces of bread instead of using forks and spoons. He had brought takeout menus to give to everyone.

Tamara had started taking ballet, as Nora had predicted. She did some graceful pirouettes to a short piece of classical music. She didn't wear a tutu, though, just a leotard and a flowy skirt.

Two kids had adopted new pets—a dog for one and a cat for the other. Coach Joe had said no pets could come to school for the party, so the pet adopters collected their oohs and ahhs by showing pictures of their new family members. Nora had a tingle of happiness, thinking about Cassidy.

When it was Amy's turn, she had a PowerPoint called "The Escape Artist."

"This is Fred," the first slide read, with a picture of the snake in its terrarium.

Some kids—including Emma—gave shrieks at the sight of Amy's new pet. Others called out, "Cool!"

The next slide showed the empty terrarium, with the caption, "GONE!"

Slides of Amy's messy room followed with the caption, "Where is Fred???"

Then: "Under the bed!"

The rest of the slides showed the terrarium, empty once again; Amy's mother looking horrified; then Fred found again; and finally a picture of Fred released, slithering into the bushes in Amy's backyard. Amy's mother had agreed to pose for the photo once Fred was found for the last time and back in the wild. Mrs. Talia never got as angry about anything as Amy thought she would.

"Nicely done, Amy!" Coach Joe said, when the laughter had died down.

Nora had expected Elise's new thing would be a new kind of writing—maybe writing a play, or a script for a movie—but Elise's new thing was gymnastics, demonstrated with one forward and one backward roll.

When Brody's turn came to show the new things he had done, he opened up a three-paneled display board like the ones kids used for science fair projects. On the board, he listed the fifty—yes, fifty—new things he had done, complete with pictures of most of them. In the center was a huge picture of Brody up in the hot-air balloon. His parents had let him do it after all.

For good measure, Brody counted to ten in French, German, Spanish, and Swahili.

He would have done an Irish jig and juggled three balls—"I usually drop them right away, but there's a couple of seconds where they're all in the air!"—but Coach Joe told him there wasn't time, given that so many students were waiting to share.

Brody pulled the next name out of the mitt: "Emma."

Emma jumped up, pulling Nora with her.

"We're doing ours together," Emma said. "Because my new thing is Nora, and Nora's new thing is me!"

Doing new things is good for your brain. New experiences build connections in your brain that keep it strong and healthy—almost like lifting weights or running on a racetrack inside your head.

16

Emma did most of the talking; Emma liked to talk more than Nora did. She explained how Nora had gotten a wonderful new cat and Emma had gotten a terrible new haircut, but their biggest new thing was how they had a big misunderstanding and made up afterward, and now she and Nora were better friends than they had ever been before.

"Even though we're opposites," Emma said, fluffing her short, cute blond curls. "Or maybe *because* we're opposites. We had *two* sleepovers, and the second one was more fun than the first. And look at Nora's French braid! I made it! And look at Nora's nails! I did them for her!"

Nora held up ten sparkly nails for all to see.

"And here's the best part. Yes, it's a cat video!"

Emma played the video of Precious Cupcake's facial on the big screen. Everyone laughed when they saw it, even though it had been funnier to see it in real life.

"Actually," Emma said, "we have *two* cat videos!"

Emma showed Nora's video of Cassidy trying to get a drink of water from the dripping kitchen faucet and tumbling into the sink. The class roared with laughter at that one, too.

"Excellent, girls!" Coach Joe said. "I'm proud of both of you."

Nora thought his smile was especially warm as it fell on her.

"Are you still giving a prize for the King and Queen of the New?" Emma asked him. "If you do, and you pick me as queen, you should pick Nora, too. We'd be co-queens."

"Well," Coach Joe said, "now that I've seen so many terrific projects, I think I'd have to give a crown to every single one."

Emma looked disappointed. Then she whispered

to Nora, "If he did give out crowns, Brody would be king, and you and I would be co-queens. I know we would!"

A few more kids presented—a new sport (fencing), a new skateboard trick, a new favorite cartoon, a new state visited on a weekend trip down to New Mexico.

Dunk's new thing turned out to be playing the violin!

"I'm going to play a song for you now," Dunk said. "I'm dedicating it to someone in our class, but I'm not going to say who it is."

Emma blushed.

The song sounded terrible. A badly played violin sounded even worse than a badly played clarinet. But Nora though she could recognize it as "Twinkle, Twinkle, Little Star." Maybe all beginners mangled the same song.

Emma beamed.

Finally it was Mason's turn.

"I haven't done a new thing," Mason confessed. "I mean, I haven't done a new thing *yet*. I'm going to do my new thing now, for the first time in the life of Mason, right here in front of you."

"Oh, my," Coach Joe said. "Team, this is an honor."

"For my new thing," Mason said, "I'm going to eat a cookie that is not a Fig Newton."

Coach Joe pounded out a drumroll on his desk.

"And it's not another regular cookie, like an Oreo or a Girl Scout cookie. It's a homemade cookie. Made by my mother, who puts things like carrots or zucchini or wheat germ, whatever that is, into everything. So this is a carrot–zucchini–wheat germ cookie. I'm not sure I'll eat the whole thing, but I'll eat at least one bite."

Coach Joe started up his drumroll again.

Mason took a bite of the cookie.

He made a terrible face at the first taste.

He chewed.

He swallowed.

The class cheered.

Nora walked home from school alone that day, hurrying to greet Cassidy, who came to the door now to meet her. The trees that had been in blossom a few weeks ago were in full leaf. The stiff, warm breeze would have ruffled her hair, but it was kept neat in her Emma-made braid.

Emma's friendship bracelet clung in tatters to Nora's wrist, hanging by one last thread. Nora rubbed it gently, remembering the day Emma had fastened it on. Nora had wanted to use it to wish Emma would give up on her as a project. But she had never been Emma's project at all; she had just been Emma's friend.

At that moment, the final frayed thread gave way. The bracelet slipped off, instantly carried by a gust of wind, sailing away toward the bare dirt of a vacant lot a block from Nora's house.

Let it go, Nora told herself.

Instead, she dashed after it.

She had trouble seeing where it had blown, but then she spied it, snagged on a weed. Nora picked it up and tucked it safely into her pocket.

Then her eyes glimpsed a small mound of dirt a few feet away.

Nora recognized the shape of that mound.

It was an anthill.

Slowly, Nora approached. Yes, ants were scurrying about, like the ants from her poor dead colony except these were full of life and activity on this perfect spring afternoon.

Nora carefully excavated the outer layers of dirt, feeling only a bit guilty about making more work for the ants that had toiled so long to create their structure of chambers and tunnels.

She knew what she would find before she found it. Somehow she knew.

There, in a deep chamber within the mound, was one ant much larger than the others, an ant born to breed generations of worker ants, an ant that could only be their queen.

"Your Majesty," Nora whispered.

Oh, this was the newest, the most wonderful new thing for an ant-loving girl! She would have her ant farm again, with an ant colony that could live forever.

As Nora gently gathered the queen and a good population of her colony into the collecting jar she kept stuffed in the bottom of her bulging backpack, she had one more thought.

She, Nora, was an ant scientist—a myrmecologist—and always would be.

But she also had a beloved cat.

And she was a poet who might publish a book of poems someday.

She had turned out to be a twisty, turny person after all.

The fingers screwing the lid back onto the ant jar sparkled brightly because of someone Nora had misjudged so badly. After all the times she had thought Emma was unscientific for believing in astrology and wishing bracelets, and for talking to seeds and singing to plants, she, Nora, had turned out to be the really unscientific one, getting such a wrong idea and holding on to it for so long, despite all the evidence to the contrary.

It was silly to give ants names. But spring was a good time for sweet silliness.

She held up the jar, where the largest ant was hidden behind her swarming subjects.

"Today," Nora said, "I christen thee Queen Emma."

Ant queens have one of the longest life spans of any insect. Some ant queens live 20 or even 30 years. That feels like forever to me. ☺

ACKNOWLEDGMENTS

To paraphrase a beloved Beatles song, every author gets by with a little help from her friends. I'm glad to have the chance to thank a few of mine here. This third book in the Nora Notebooks series wouldn't have existed without the vision of its first wonderful editor, Nancy Hinkel. Now that she is off pursuing exciting adventures that would make Coach Joe proud, my new editor, Julia Maguire, offered brilliant insights to shape the book into its final form. Katie Kath outdoes herself in each new title, with even more adorable illustrations. Thanks also to my constantly supportive and encouraging agent, Steve Fraser; to fabulously careful proofreader Marianne Cohen; to Isabel Warren-Lynch and Trish Parcell for their appealing book design; to Stephen Brown for chiming in with helpful editorial suggestions that strengthened the book considerably;

and to Barbara Fisch and Sarah Shealy at Blue Slip Media for being the best publicists in the world for the series. Hooray for friends, old and new, who help authors plant, water, weed, fertilize, and harvest their garden of books in ever new and wondrous ways.

ABOUT THE AUTHOR

Claudia Mills is the author of over fifty books for young readers, including the Mason Dixon series. She does not personally keep an ant farm, but she does have a cat, Snickers, with whom she curls up on her couch at home in Boulder, Colorado, drinking hot chocolate and writing. Visit her at claudiamillsauthor.com.